LIVING DEATH

DEATH'S DOORSTEP SERIES

MIA HALL

DEDICATION

Thank you to the readers! You've made my dragon dreams a reality!

Sign up for Mia's Newsletter to find out about new releases.

Put the following in your browser window: mailerlite.com/webforms/landing/e1d4k4

Covers by Ammonia Book Covers

❧   I   ❧

The crunching gravel under Kiera's car, or rather her parents' car, gave way to a smooth, freshly paved road as her father pulled up in front of the Dreadmore Academy grounds gate. The tall white pillars and black metal bars that protected the facility from intruders no longer looked as intimidating as they had almost six months ago. Now, Kiera felt a sense of calm and familiarity as she looked beyond them at the massive trees with their unnaturally green leaves. The ground behind them and the miles of land they had passed were covered in day-old snow, and the only trees bearing leaves were pine. Beyond this gate, however, everything was green and bright. There was still a chill that zipped through the car window as her father lowered it to speak to the guard. Flowers littered the ground, and their petals were just as bright and colorful now as they would be in spring.

Her father hadn't changed much in Kiera's six months away. He still had his black hair, combed back with a bit too much gel, something he picked up in his younger years and never let go of. He kept running his hands through it nervously as the guard in a blue and white uniform asked him for an ID and proof of Kiera's enrollment at the magical academy.

Her mother, seated on the passenger side, kept leaning over to speak over her father since his nervous voice was too quiet to be heard clearly over the wind.

While Kiera's father gave off a very dark, brooding impression with his dark hair and eyes, as well as dark clothes that covered every inch of his skin, her mother was all sunshine and professionalism. Her blond hair was curled perfectly, and her fingernails matched the red of her lipstick. One would think the magic-wielder in the family would be the one acting and looking all mysterious and wearing long, dark robes. Instead, her mother, the one who used necromancy to investigate murders, was the bright one.

Sadly, Kiera never learned to take after her

mother's grooming and taste in clothes. Just like her father, her hair and eyes were deep brown, and her clothing of choice consisted of jeans, sweats, tees or sweaters, and white or black tennis shoes. She would occasionally throw on a pair of good running shoes for a hike or gym activity, but Dreadmore didn't make gym classes mandatory like the normal school did, so she hadn't touched those shoes in months.

"Yes, my daughter's name is Kiera Tully," her mother proclaimed loudly to the guard as he accepted their IDs. "She's the one who caught that serial killer two months ago."

Kiera blanched, praying her mother wouldn't make some comment about how Kiera "did the security's job for them." She didn't want the guards to think badly of her. They would be the ones looking out for her, after all. Though, to be fair, they really hadn't done a great job with that "serial killer," as her mother called it. The criminal would have succeeded in her murder if Kiera and her *not-quite* boyfriend hadn't stumbled across her.

Thankfully, the guard handed back the IDs before her mother could say any more, and Kiera breathed a sigh of relief.

"Welcome back to Dreadmore, Miss Tully." The security guard tipped his blue hat to her and motioned for the car to move forward once the gate was open. The smile he gave Kiera seemed genuine, so she hoped perhaps he was grateful she'd helped out two months ago. That or he was just being nice.

Her father's own sigh of relief sounded identical to Kiera's as he rolled up the window and tapped his fingers on the steering wheel, watching as the gate slowly inched open on both sides. Her mother peered forward at the mechanism controlling the gates, whistling slightly.

"Reliant on magic," she said quietly.

"How?" her father asked, sounding a little tired from the trip. Since he was never a magic user, everything she said often went over his head.

"A movement spell, combined with heat magic of some kind." Her mother was nodding to herself, hmming as though it should be obvious. Now Kiera was studying the gates too, not sure how it was magic. All she saw were the pillars connected to the gates.

"Seems a bit risky to make everything reliant on magic, doesn't it?" her father asked quietly. "What if something happens that makes everyone lose their magic? You'd be trapped."

Kiera had inherited his paranoia too.

"Hush." Her mom shook her head and glanced

back at Kiera. "Don't worry, dear. That won't happen. It would be next to impossible to create a magic-free zone in an area this large. If the gates can't be used, the professors can just cut a hole in the wall or something."

Kiera nodded. "I wasn't worried about it."

"Yes, Howard, she wasn't worried about it, so don't put those thoughts into her head," her mother said, turning her attention back to her ex-husband. Any discussion of magic caused friction between them, to the point where even Kiera got tired of listening.

Magic wasn't the only reason her parents got divorced, and Kiera's own presence wasn't the only reason they were together in the car now, but she still hated hearing her parents discuss magic at all now. It always led to her father questioning the risks and morality of it and her mother defending necromancy to her last breath.

Shoving a stray strand of hair out of her face, Kiera rolled down her own window so she could watch the scenery and ignore her parents as they continued discussing the security of the school.

Her winter break, which had been extended due to early school closure, had carried with it the strong smell of pine, sap, wet snow, and mint. Now, in a matter of minutes, those scents and the snow that came with it had literally melted away. It gave way to the bright greens of spring, as well as the fresh scent of wet mud and growing grass coupled together. Birds flew by, chirping cheerfully at the sky, and a few butterflies flitted about on the glowing flowers that shouldn't be growing at this time of year. A stray beetle even flew through the window and landed on Kiera's leg, taking a moment to rest on her jeans.

Deja-vu overcame her as she recalled a similar creature flying around her car the first time she came here. That one had been green and ended up burnt to a crisp due to her attempts at necromancy. She'd been desperate to assess her skills and see if she had what it took to make it in Dreadmore without embarrassing herself.

Now, she didn't need to worry about that anymore.

Smiling slightly at the irony of the situation, she put the tip of her finger under the black bug's body, waited for it to climb on with its numerous legs, then released it into the free air again.

"All I'm saying is, there needs to be a balance," her father was saying, his tone implying that the discussion would end after this final sentence. "Magic users should have a proper blend of both practical and magical devices, so they don't become reliant on one or the other."

It was clear by the quiet scoff her mother made that she had plenty of things to say about that, but both she and Kiera knew how to read his social cues, so she dropped it. Instead, her mom turned toward Kiera and poked her leg playfully.

"So, will we be seeing this boy when we drop you off?" she asked, a cheeky grin on her normally serious, stoic face. "I can hop out for a few minutes to introduce myself. I'd love to meet him."

Kiera cringed inwardly. They were referring, of course, to Ezra Gillis. He was the son of a prestigious family, and his uncle was the headmaster of this very academy. She got to know him last semester through their "love of studying," as she liked to call it, and when he was nearly killed by the vengeful woman who kept freezing playboys on campus, Kiera ended up saving him. Although they weren't officially dating or anything, they had kept in contact throughout the entire winter break, and Kiera knew that at least she was falling hard for him every day. She hoped he felt the same, but there was no way she'd be telling her parents that.

"He's just a friend," she said, for what felt like the tenth time since Christmas vacation began.

"You haven't insisted on meeting any of my other friends."

"I have plenty of friends," her father said without turning away from the road. "They don't text me every couple of minutes for two months straight."

Kiera felt heat rise up the back of her neck and onto the tips of her ears. She thought she'd been subtle when texting Ezra. She'd tried to avoid messaging him when family was around.

"Oh, I can tell this is more than a friend," her mother added mischievously. "The look on your face when Ben texted you was completely different from this other boy."

"If we ever start dating, you can meet with him," Kiera cut in quickly, wanting to end this torment immediately. "Until then, he is just a friend, and I don't want you doing anything... embarrassing."

"How could you say that, Kiera?" her mother gasped sarcastically, putting her hand to her mouth and everything. "My own daughter that I carried for nine months thinks I'm embarrassing? Her own mother?"

Despite being eighteen years old now, Kiera still felt like she was ten years younger when her mother acted like this. It made her want to curl up and pout as she did at that age. Sadly, such things weren't allowed now, not in her eyes at least.

"Just let me be for now," she said, keeping her voice low and betraying no emotion. That blush would not be allowed to creep all the way onto her cheeks. "You wouldn't want to scare him away and mess things up for me, would you?" she added with a raised eyebrow.

"Ah." Her mother pointed at Kiera and chuckled. "She's gotten too smart for her own good. She knows how eager I am for grandchildren and doesn't want me to—"

"Mom!" *Who said anything about grandchildren?*

All maturity went out the window, and Kiera turned toward the window in a huff, ignoring her mother's teasing laughter as they reached the end of their journey.

"Well, if you and that boy do start dating, make sure you let me know," her mother said, kinder this time and not making jokes at her daughter's expense.

Kiera bit her lip and nodded. "Thanks, Mom."

"That way, your father can go after the boy with a shotgun if he isn't deemed worthy of my daughter," her mother finished.

"Mom, I swear—"

Her mother just laughed, getting the last

sarcastic dig in before they pulled off the road and into the academy parking lot. "Don't worry," her mom said, tears forming as her chuckling subsided. "We won't do anything embarrassing. I save my teasing for moments like this."

Kiera knew she meant it, so she didn't protest again. She had other things to worry about anyway, like finishing her second semester and passing the exams that would make her an official member of the school. Her chances of gaining a prestigious degree that would grant her any necromancy-related job she wanted hinged on this semester. If she failed now, her dreams of using magic to heal others would feel that much farther away.

Luckily, things didn't feel as hopeless this time as they did last semester. Unless something exceedingly horrible happened, as her father feared, there was nothing to worry about.

❧ 2 ☙

It became clear as they pulled into the expansive parking lot in front of the academy buildings that a renovation had been made over the winter break. Whether this was done practically, with real brick and wood, or through the use of magic, Kiera couldn't tell. Perhaps her mother could, but Kiera didn't care enough to ask.

The huge staff building was the first thing someone entering would see. It used to consist of red stone that gave it an older but academic look. Now, it had been changed into something akin to a tall, grey castle with gargoyles and shingles and even one tower where the bell used to hang. From what Kiera could see, the other buildings had been given a similar makeover, though they looked a little more practical.

"Are we sure we came to the right place?" her father asked as he put the car into park.

His attempt at a joke didn't mask his nerves. His voice was shaking, and Kiera could see his hands doing the same as he turned off the engine. He probably didn't like seeing so much change at once. It was yet another reminder of how powerful magic could be and how only a small part of the population could use it. That put ordinary people like himself at a huge disadvantage. Luckily, her mother didn't catch his apprehension this time.

"I assume they change things up, so the students have something to tell their parents," her mother replied. "Keeps the mystery and prestige intact, perhaps?"

"Maybe." Her father shrugged and got out of the car. "I'll get your bags, Kiera."

"Thanks." Kiera ignored how the renovation made her slightly more nervous since so much change at once dampened the welcome feeling of returning. Instead, she focused on climbing out of the car and helping her dad pull her backpack and two suitcases from the car. She'd brought more this time than the last since now she actually expected to stay here for four years rather than getting expelled two months in for failing grades. She'd brought more clothes and books from home in the hope that it would make her dorm feel more permanent and homey.

After she had her bags positioned so she could pull them all at once, her dad gave her a hug goodbye and told her, just like last time, to call him if anything went wrong. She didn't the last time things went downhill and could tell by his downcast eyes and slumped shoulders that he wished she had.

Perhaps he thought his lack of magic made him seem untrustworthy or unable to protect her. That wasn't the case. She hadn't felt like anyone, even the highest magic users at the school, could help, so she hadn't wanted to worry her parents.

"I will," she assured him, honest this time, and gave him a second hug in the hopes that it would reassure him.

Her mother leaned out the car window for her hug, then nudged Kiera and pointed at the other end of the parking lot, near the steps leading up to the staff building. "I see Ben over there. Which one of those two boys is the one?" She wiggled her eyebrows and didn't get a reaction from Kiera.

Kiera looked the way her mother had pointed and, sure enough, Ben, Ezra, and Tucker were standing together, chatting. They'd become good friends over the semester, thanks in part to Kiera. She was the glue that bound them together, in a way, so it felt odd to see them having fun without her.

Ben was dressed in green pants, which looked a little silly, and a sky-blue top. His blond hair had streaks of blue in it now, and they matched his outfit. The color seemed a little juvenile on him since he was fully grown now and looked like an adult from afar. Blue hair suited his personality, though, so Kiera just shrugged it off. He was wildly throwing his hands about as he described something, possibly the holidays, to an amused Tucker and suspicious Ezra. Knowing Ezra, he knew by this point how Ben liked to exaggerate and dramatize everything.

Tucker, Ezra's best friend, was the tallest of the three and had the biggest smile. He was currently laughing at something Ben said, his darker skin offset by the bright red shirt he was wearing. His hair also had the most care put into it and was a pleasant deep brown. It looked especially good next to Ben's obnoxious blue.

Ezra stood out the most among the three of them, though. That might just be Kiera's bias since she'd had a crush on him since the first time she laid eyes on him, but objectively he was quite good-looking anyway.

He was wearing a deep green, matching Tucker's

red to create a Christmas vibe, and his brown hair was a mix between curly and wavy today. The gauntness of his cheeks and bags under his eyes, which had developed due to his worries about the serial killer, were gone. Instead, he had a full face, and his jaw seemed even stronger. He might have hit the final part of his growth spurt while he was away if that was even a thing. Kiera didn't understand how boys grew by this point.

"I think I can already tell which one it is," her mother said, interrupting Kiera's study of the three boys.

"Oh? Because you know his parents?" Kiera asked. Ezra's parents were part of the top 1% of magic-wielders in America. Her mother had definitely at least heard of them.

"No. Because of the way you look at him," her mother said sappily before patting her on the arm and leaning back in her seat. "Be good. Take care of yourself. Please call me at least every week, okay, and if there are any serial killers about, make sure you inform me right away."

Kiera couldn't help laughing at that last part. Without context, it sounded like a very odd request. "I will."

After waving goodbye, her parents were gone. Kiera hoped they wouldn't start arguing again in her absence but forced the thought out of her mind as she approached her friends. It was clear by this point that their conversation had veered away from Ben's sporadic stories to something more sobering because none of them looked happy now. Even Tucker's smile had morphed into a frown.

As she studied Ezra, who hadn't spotted her yet, she realized that he hadn't looked grumpy because of Ben's ridiculous stories. His crossed arms and furrowed brow seemed more permanent the closer she got. Something was wrong, either with him or their surroundings. She couldn't tell which.

"Hey," she said hesitantly as she walked up to the group. "Everything okay?"

Ben and Tucker's conversation ended abruptly, and their smiles returned as they moved forward to hug her, but Ezra's expression didn't change. It made her heart drop as he not only didn't smile, but his eyes seemed to darken at the sight of her. Something was seriously wrong.

After she hugged Ben and Tucker hello, updating them on everything that had happened over the break—which wasn't much—she stepped forward to give Ezra a hug too. As he pulled her close and she felt his entire body tensing, she whispered, "Is something wrong?" in his ear. It was something she didn't want Tucker or Ben to hear.

But as he pulled away and she felt his arms grip hers for just a little too long, he shook his head. "No. Nothing's wrong," he said quietly. Then, he promised to talk to her later, waved goodbye to their other two friends, and walked off to join the parade of students walking past the staff building and heading toward the dorms.

Butterflies flew through her stomach as he turned away, but the insects quickly turned to lead inside her, and she felt her heart twist painfully. He wasn't okay. He was acting almost as bad as he did during Tucker's attempted murder. He hadn't mentioned anything being wrong when he texted her yesterday to wish her luck on the trip here. What could have happened between then and now?

Kiera turned back to her best friend and squinted at him. "Did you do something to him, Ben?" she asked accusingly. Sometimes Ben put his foot in his mouth. In the past, he'd accidentally joked about Ezra's family without realizing it.

Ben raised his arms in defense and took a dramatic step back. "I am innocent. I've done nothing."

Hopefully, Ezra was just nervous about reentering the school. Either the fear of a new life-threatening situation had him on edge, or his family's expectations were wearing down on him again.

Either way, she'd ask him in person or over text by the end of the day.

As Ben continued defending himself, Tucker tilted his head ever so slightly, implying he knew what might be going on. Once Ben stopped talking, he finally let them in on what was going on.

Students weaved around the trio as they hunched together to talk. Kiera noticed more of the same magical types passing by that she'd seen last time she was here. There were invisible people slipping through the crowd, only noticeable because the sun reflected off them and warped the air around them. There were also people buffed or prettied up with magic to make them more attractive or impressive. Some had familiars hanging on their shoulders. Others had discolored eyes or brightly colored hair designed to match the outfit they were wearing. Kiera was surprised the school didn't have a section designated solely for those using their magic to make people more beautiful or fashionable. There had to be money in it.

Tucker lowered his voice as he pulled Ben and Kiera closer so their conversation could be private enough. Then, he licked his lips nervously and spoke.

"You two know about Ezra's family already, right? And all their prestige?"

Kiera nodded. She knew how much pressure his family name put on him.

Ben nodded too. He had once criticized the headmaster, Ezra's uncle, right in front of Ezra and came to regret it.

"Well, Ezra isn't the only one studying necromancy," Tucker said, surprising Kiera. If she recalled correctly, the reason Ezra's parents pushed him so hard was that all his older siblings went into fields outside magic. Did he lie to her?

"He has an elder brother named Kent," Tucker continued quietly. "And we just heard today that Kent is going to be teaching here for the semester."

Kiera felt jitters in her stomach. Ezra had already mentioned not liking the family ties, and she was sure having the headmaster keep an eye on your studies and grades was nerve-wracking. Now there'd be a second family member watching him too? That must have been what put him in such a horrid mood.

"And I've only met Kent once in passing, but he

isn't the nicest fellow," Tucker finished, warily scanning the perimeter to make sure the man in question wasn't around to hear. "So don't be offended if Ezra seems off or quiet. I think he's just adjusting to the reality. I'm sure he'll get better in no time." Tucker flashed both of them a wide grin, his perfectly straight teeth doing little to put Kiera at ease.

"Is there anything we can do for him?" Kiera asked, even though she already knew the answer was no. When Tucker confirmed it, she just nodded sullenly and looked up at the staff building. She had hoped this was her chance to finalize her relationship with Ezra. Now that he had other things on his mind, she knew dating was the last thing he'd be worried about.

"Thanks for letting us know," Ben said. "I was a little worried I pissed him off and didn't know why."

"I mean, if it weren't for Kent, you probably would be the reason he was pissed off," Tucker joked. "I'm kidding. Don't worry. It's not like this is the first time he's dealt with family intervention and a lack of boundaries. Unless his family starts prying into any of our lives too, I think it's best to stay out of it."

"Will do," Ben said, a little too eagerly. While

Kiera knew Ben liked Ezra well enough, he clearly didn't want to deal with any more members of the Gillis family. Ben liked to think of himself as rebellious, though he never went further than napping in class, and every member of the Gillis family seemed to be some type of authority figure. That wouldn't match with Ben's view of himself.

"We'll just ask him if he needs any help during dinner," Kiera suggested, still a little worried about him. He'd looked stressed and agitated. It wasn't quite as bad as when Tucker's life was in danger but even still...

"Good idea," Tucker replied, but she could tell he didn't think it would do any good. He'd clearly resigned himself to letting Ezra's issues take care of themselves. Unfortunately for Kiera, if she wanted to date him in the future, family would become part of it. So, she had no choice.

Unfortunately, when all four of them met up for dinner in the cafeteria that evening, as had become a habit by this point, Ezra clearly wasn't feeling much better.

Kiera kept an eye on him as she sat down across from him, next to Ben. The tables had changed from blue plastic to black wood, yet another magical renovation done during the Christmas break. To celebrate students returning for their second semester, they were served a traditional Christmas meal of turkey, gravy, mashed potatoes, green beans and corn, and a dessert of many different pies. All of it tasted divine. There was also a man in the corner, juggling an obscene number of live birds to entertain the students. He was wearing a Santa outfit but without a beard, and it made for a very strange but funny sight.

Unfortunately, Ezra didn't even look the juggler's way as he put his silver tray on the table and dug in silently. There was zero eye contact from him for the first ten minutes of the meal, in which Tucker and Ben attempted to start a group conversation about the holidays but eventually dwindled to silence.

After twenty minutes of hearing nothing from Ezra, she finally decided to put in some effort and rouse him. He wasn't feeling like himself, and it had all of them nervous.

"How were your holidays, Ezra?" She already knew the answer since they texted the whole time but couldn't think of any stimulating conversation starters at the moment.

Ezra looked up slowly, eyes glazed over, then blinked a few times and forced his lips upward in a poor attempt at a smile. "Same as usual. Just visiting family and everything." His tone of voice deepened at the word *family*. "Tell me about yours." He directed this to all three of them, then slumped down again once the other boys started speaking. His time to talk was over, and Kiera could already see him retreating into his own thoughts again.

She pursed her lips, wanting to reach forward and grasp his hand to let him know he wasn't alone.

But now didn't feel like the right time, with Ben and Tucker right there, so she left Ezra alone and vowed to text him about his issues tonight. Hopefully, he'd open up to her like he did last semester.

✣ 4 ✣

Kiera did end up texting Ezra, telling him how great it was to see him again and attempting to ask how he was without being overly nosy. However, his response was minimal.

I'm fine. Just adjusting to school again. Can we sit at the front of class together tomorrow?

She had to admit that his request warmed her heart a little. Not only was he expecting to sit beside her without question, something that felt so unreachable at the start of last semester, but he was asking first because he knew she liked sitting in the middle. The front always made her feel vulnerable. Everyone in the class could be staring at the back of her head, and she'd have no way of knowing.

Of course, she replied, then sighed.

He'd dodged her question, or rather just gave the simple answer that didn't really mean anything at all. "Fine" was the same as saying nothing. But that made it clear he didn't want to talk about it and was her sign to lay off. If he wanted to talk to her about his family, he'd do it on his own time. Her job was to just stay by his side and help brighten things up.

So, the next day, when she followed the courses on her class schedule and found her first necromancy class, Ezra was already at the front of the classroom to the right. Like last semester, this class was more of a lecture hall. The walls were a deep red wood, and the long, row seats matched. This time, rather than simply being hard chairs that made your legs numb by the end of class, these had soft-looking, red satin cushions on them. The renovation didn't look too bad now.

A few other students were seated already, a few of whom she recognized from last semester, including some girls who used to (probably) be jealous of her friendship with Ezra. There were still ten minutes before class, so Kiera wouldn't know how many were in attendance until much later. The professor wasn't here either. She'd noticed his name wasn't listed for this class, which either meant the professor hadn't been decided yet or there was a sudden change. That happened last semester when the original professor got pregnant and left right after the first day of school, so another took her place. She wished it would be her professor from last year, Professor Smith, who was very kind and helpful but knew she shouldn't get her hopes up.

"Hey," she said as she slid in next to him, ignoring how her voice cracked. "I just saw that the professor for this class is unlisted," she said.

Ezra nodded, looking up from the textbook he'd been reading. It was called *Speaking to the Dead* and was something her mother would have read. He was already on page forty.

She continued, "Who do you think it will be? I'm hoping it'll be Professor Smith."

"Me too." He leaned back as far as he could on the seat, stretching, and naturally draped his arm around her shoulder as he did so. It was so smooth, she didn't notice until she felt his hand squeeze her arm gently. "He was a good guy. I still love remembering the shock on his face when you sent that bird flying through the maze."

As she pulled her books from her bag, she settled in and relished the warm feeling of comfort and security being next to Ezra brought her. Things felt normal again until loud footsteps echoed down the hall, and their new professor stepped through the door. It wasn't Professor Smith. This man was much younger, with chestnut brown hair that curled around his brow and a white lab coat that felt like it belonged to a scientist rather than a magic-practicer or a professor. He had some loose folders under his shoulder and slammed them on the professor's desk at the front of the room, in front of the chalkboards and screens. As he made his presence known with his loud actions, he studied each of their faces before finally landing on Ezra's. Kiera felt Ezra's hand withdraw from her shoulder, and she felt his body tense up too. As soon as he did so, she realized who exactly this professor was. No wonder his face felt slightly familiar. He looked like an older version of Ezra.

It was Kent, Ezra's eldest sibling. He was to be their homeroom professor.

5

Kiera felt her entire body tense up. Her toes pushed into the front of her shoes, her eyes remained straight ahead, and her back pushed up against the wooden part of the long seat. All the while, she watched this new professor. The longer she looked, the less he looked like Ezra. While their appearances were, on the surface, very similar, there was something about the way they carried themselves and how their expressions formed on their faces that was different.

Where Ezra was guarded at first but able to smile easily and more than happy to crack a joke at the right time, this Kent person had a perpetual scowl, which only went away when he turned to the rest of the class and tightened his face up. His eyes squinted, his lips turned upwards, and he eventually showed his teeth, but it was clearly a poor imitation of a smile that was meant to look jovial and natural. Kiera knew it wasn't. He didn't like any of them. Why? She couldn't be sure.

The sense of comfort her favorite, Professor Smith, had brought was gone. Replaced by it were a racing heart and constant worry about how she looked. All the anxiety she thought she'd gotten over from last semester had returned, except this time it was a reaction to the professor, not the students.

"I trust you all enjoyed your break," the professor said, his booming voice nearly making the floor shake. His voice was much deeper than Ezra's, though maybe Ezra's would sound that way eventually. "But don't expect another until the semester is over and you've passed your exams. If I catch any one of you not paying attention or goofing off during class, I will not hesitate to give you a zero without warning."

Kiera's eyes widened, as many others surely did. There were a few gasps.

Then one person spoke up. "You can't do that!"

"I can and I will." His tone of voice made Kiera believe it too. "Just look up my name, and you'll know why I have that power. Now sit up straight and turn to page—"

Kiera did as he instructed, following along with the lesson and sweating the entire time. She'd occasionally glance at Ezra and would see him clutching his pencil so tight it looked ready to break. His jaw was in a similar situation. It must be so frustrating to not only be taught by your own brother but also have him act like such a condescending jerk. Now Kiera was beginning to understand why the two had so much tension.

Despite constantly shouting to be heard and asking hard questions that would result in a judgmental glare if the answering student got it wrong, Kent was fairly good at teaching. Just like Ezra was with her, Kent understood the magic inside and out, which made him an expert at explaining things in a way that was easy to understand. It was clear he was passionate about necromancy, though he'd sometimes get a dark glint in his eyes when talking about death.

By the end of class, Kiera felt exhausted despite doing nothing but listening. She wasn't sure she'd be able to survive an entire semester with this professor. At least it was only one class a day, though.

"Pack up quickly," she whispered to Ezra once class was over, and the professor's back was turned. "I want out of here."

Ezra's pale face said the same, but as soon as they stood up, Kent turned around and leveled a long stare at his little brother. Ezra froze, staring at the ground and clenching his jaw again. Kiera did the same, feeling like a deer caught in the headlights.

"Don't leave yet, Ezra," Kent said. His voice was significantly quieter now, compared to him practically shouting for the entire hour-long lesson, but it still held a bite siblings shouldn't normally have. "I need to talk to you." He nodded at Kiera, dismissing her, then sat down at his desk and rested his hands on top of it. The look he gave Kiera was a questioning one, trying to figure out why she hadn't immediately left when he told her to.

"I'll see you at lunch," she whispered to Ezra, sweating again and wishing she could run to the dorm to get a change of clothes. Then, feeling like she'd abandoned him, she grabbed her full book bag and made for the door as quickly as possible without running. She didn't look at Ezra as she left, knowing she'd immediately feel guilty if she did. She already knew the sad, dejected look he'd have on his face—that or he'd have zero expression like his brother had stolen his soul and left only the fleshy shell behind. She wasn't sure which was worse.

She vowed to ask Ezra about his brother and what she could do to help, but as she turned around at the door and took one more look at the siblings, she doubted Ezra would tell her anything.

Just as she feared, Ezra looked completely out of it. His eyes had glazed over, and he was standing at attention like a toy soldier, awaiting orders. The brother, meanwhile, had a real smile this time. His lips were turned up like a Cheshire cat's, and the evil grin didn't reach his eyes.

"You may go, Miss Tully," Kent said without even looking at her. He clearly wouldn't start talking until she left. All the other students had already booked it, eager to get away.

Kiera tried to say okay, but she was so nervous, she made no sound. So she just stepped back into the hall and shut the door behind her.

"Traitor," she muttered to herself for abandoning Ezra, even though there was nothing she could have done. "Some girlfriend you'd make."

6

Her next classes proceeded normally. She didn't have any friends in any of them, but the girl she sat next to forgot her textbook, so they shared and ended up chatting about their interests in different types of healing magic. It wasn't so bad. The girl even promised to sit together next time. Things were looking up.

But then, when Kiera went to lunch, Ezra wasn't there, and he didn't answer her texts until after all the classes were done. He said he just got busy, and when she asked if they could meet afterward, he said he was tired and would be turning in early, so she assumed he went back to his dorm for the night.

That left an overly concerned Kiera alone since

Tucker and Ben were off doing their own things, and now she had a lot of time to herself.

So, she did what she always did last semester. She headed to the library, loaded up with all her textbooks, and found a spot to study.

Unlike most of the other buildings and rooms, the library was unchanged. Only the walls had been moved and repainted to a deep, natural wood brown. The rest of the building, from the book-shelves and computers to the librarian's desk, was the same. Everything was simple, efficient, and had the musty smell of old books mixed with new, freshly printed ones. There was a quiet hum of whispered conversation, and because it was the first day, most of the seats were empty, so Kiera's favorite chair in one of the corners was still empty and surrounded by the cocoon of bookshelves.

She'd become fairly good at practicing spells without actually letting the spells do anything, at least on paper. It was simple. All one had to do was skip the keywords. That's what normal people did, at least. However, with her, magic felt a little more volatile. Even if she said a spell correctly, sometimes the magic seemed to have a mind of its own, and it would take the messed-up spell and turn it into something else. She'd gotten a hold of it now, for the most part, but it still felt risky to practice in public. So, the most she would do was say the spells in her head where they couldn't interact with the physical world.

After about an hour of studying spells, memorizing them, and figuring out how the components interacted with the spell, she was exhausted. Not only was it taxing to read for so long, since the words sometimes felt switched around or backward, but her mind also kept straying to Ezra. Should she text him to see if he was okay? Would he get mad if she did? Would he think she was nosy or pushing past his boundaries? They weren't dating, she had to keep reminding herself, so she should know her place.

"Fine. I give up." The words were practically spinning on the page now. She slammed it shut, cringing at how it echoed in the big, nearly empty room, then got up from her seat.

There were a few other students sitting around who looked up when she moved, but then they became uninterested and turned back to their books. Some were reading normal superhero comics, others fictional romance novels, and a few were poring over ancient texts full of magical spells. It was an interesting combo.

Comic books sounded like a promising idea, though. The pictures might offer her mind a break from all that reading. Besides, she didn't really want to go back to her dorm just yet, because she'd have even more time to think and stress about Ezra.

The comics were at the back of the library. Ezra had said he thought it was because the professors wanted students to focus on "real" books and not get distracted by the exciting superheroes and comedic shorts. Kiera partly agreed with him. The placement had certainly discouraged her from seeking them out, especially because not only did it take a full five minutes to reach them far back in the stacks, but this part of the buildings was also considerably darker. The bookshelves stretched higher up, nearly touching the ceiling, and they blocked out most of the yellow light. There was no magical light here since the space was rarely used.

A shiver ran up her back as she passed through the rows upon rows of musty books. She would occasionally pass someone creepily sitting on the floor, muttering to themselves as they read. There was even a moment when she caught movement in the corner of her eye, right behind one of the book-shelves, but turned and saw nothing. It might just be her mind playing tricks on her, or it might have been something real that used magic to conceal itself.

Either way, she wanted to grab the books fast and never come back.

Next time, she'd be sure to bring Ben with her. This place was like a second home to him. She couldn't count how many times he'd snuck back here to grab more comics when they were supposed to be studying.

Once she got to the shelves she was looking for, which were all spread out across the back wall, their bright spines and welcoming covers with smiling girls in bright dresses or superhero costumes put her at ease. In no time, she was walking back and forth along the shelves, studying each one and looking for something that could help her pass the next hour.

She eventually settled on *The Incredible Turtle Boy* and *Salamander Sam*. They looked silly enough to get her mind off things.

Then, flimsy books under her arm, she headed back. This time, instead of using the main hall that led right between both rows of bookshelves to get back, she headed back along the far wall. This way, there was something solid on her left, and she could focus all her attention on her right, lest something jump out at her. She felt a little less trapped this way.

Two minutes in, she was halfway through. Her nerves were lessoning. Her feet felt less wobbly. Everything was going great until she encountered something strange on her left, right in the wall.

She saw movement out of the corner of her eye again, but this time, when she turned, she spotted something moving on the bookshelf right next to her head. It was a small, white orb that looked like a combination of fluff and light that somehow didn't extend beyond its own body. It had no face, limbs, or other defining features and seemed to bob up and down in the air like it was floating in invisible water.

She'd never seen anything like this before and couldn't help staring. Something about it was entrancing like it felt good just to look at it. She could stare for hours, and maybe she did.

Then it started floating past her and through the bookshelves, sometimes coming to rest on a book before continuing its journey again. Something inside Kiera egged her to follow it. It felt like she'd lost something important, though she didn't know what, and perhaps the orb would lead her to it.

"This is so strange," she muttered to herself, but

her words moved on despite her mind telling her something about this was very, very wrong.

I'll just follow it for a minute. She held her chin up high as she pursued it. *Besides, it's not like I'm alone in the library.*

However, that *serial killer* from last semester did her dirty work in plain sight too.

7

The orb's journey through the library felt like a sweet, little adventure Kiera might have imagined during her childhood. The library felt ten times larger than it had an hour ago, and the hushed voices seemed to dull in her ears.

After they moved forward for nearly ten minutes, she started to seriously consider leaving the orb to its quest. They had to be going in a circle to walk this far and not reach walls or anything.

Then, she saw it.

In front of her, on the left wall where she'd originally found the orb, was a door that didn't belong. All the regular doors were tall, wooden, and had golden knockers on the front. This door, on the other hand, was a golden color. The shine had faded, and it was dark around the edges like the paint was peeling off and revealing stone or steel underneath, but it was still entrancing in its beauty. The handles of the door almost looked like hanging golden ropes, though they were clearly solid.

Most strange and intriguing was what lay on top of the door. Covering the entire exterior were leaves and flowers. Most were woven into the wood or steel, while others looked like they'd been glued on. Sadly, most of them were dead and colorless now, but the browns added to the fading gold.

Kiera desperately wanted to touch it. Something in her heart said it was the right thing to do. This door and what lay beyond it was calling to the magic inside her. It was begging her to open that door and continue the adventure. If she didn't, the mystery of what lay beyond would taunt her for the rest of her life and drive her insane.

But there was considerable risk. This door felt magical, and with magic always came risks. Just like a necromancy spell needed components to avoid the spell stealing something it shouldn't, other forms of magic had to be understood, controlled, and contained. She didn't know what this door was, why it was here, or who put it here. Opening it felt risky.

"But I must," she hissed, angry at herself for

suggesting she give up this journey and be tormented by what-ifs for eternity. "Besides, we can go anywhere in the school besides staff areas." It didn't feel strange that she was talking to herself. The orb was still floating beside her, right next to the door, so it almost felt like she was addressing it instead. "This door doesn't have a sign on it forbidding entry, so I'm allowed in."

Something about her own explanation felt sorely wrong, but she ignored that nagging feeling and touched the rope handles. Just as she thought, they were solid as rocks, merely mimicking the appearance of a rope.

As soon as her finger brushed against the rope, the door suddenly burst to life. The dead leaves turned into greens and oranges, the flowers into pinks and blues. The gold returned to its beautiful shine, and the handles softened. She thought the door was before, but now it was breathtaking.

She held her breath as the door began to slowly open on its own, allowing a thin stream of light to come through. The orb bobbed next to it, silently conveying excitement.

Kiera leaned forward, eager to see what was inside.

Then, she woke up.

KIERA AWOKE, STILL IN HER HIDDEN CORNER chair in the library. She was so surprised when she awakened that she jerked forward and nearly fell out of the seat she'd fallen asleep in. A few students sitting nearby turned to see what happened, then, when they realized nothing was wrong, turned back to their own books again.

Blinking rapidly and feeling out of breath even though she'd only been asleep, Kiera leaned back in the chair and looked at her watch. How long had she been asleep? It felt like at least three hours since she got up to look for those comics. Or maybe only one hour.

To her shock, only thirty minutes had passed since she stood up, and to make things even more confusing, she didn't have the comics with her.

It took her a moment to figure out that she hadn't gotten up to get the comics at all. She'd fallen asleep while reading her spell book, which was still open on her lap. There were no comics, no stacks, no orb, and certainly no magical flower door.

The effects of the dream still lingering and disorienting her, she quickly packed up her books and headed to her dorm room. The dream had felt so real that part of her wanted to see if the door was real, but she knew it couldn't be. Her brain must have been so desperate for entertainment and stress relief that it had fabricated some enchanted door and a little featureless fairy that led her to it. She loved books like The Secret Garden as a child, so the door in that book must have influenced her teen mind too.

Kiera huffed as she exited the library, crossed the grounds to the dorms, found her room, and dumped her books in a corner. That was more than enough reading for one day.

Ezra didn't text her back again that evening.

8

The next day, she woke up exhausted. She was sure it was a combination of stress —both from Ezra, his brother, and reentering school—as well as a strange nagging feeling from her library dream that never went away. It irked her so much that she told Ben about it during the one science class they shared together. It was, surprisingly, a magic-free class that was only offered once a year. Both of them didn't take many science classes during their regular high school years, so they figured they might as well share it.

Today they were labeling parts of the body, which was coincidentally helpful for necromancy, and since the professor let them work in pairs without interruption, it offered the perfect chance to update Ben on everything.

After she explained the dream in excruciating detail, Ben shrugged as he held his pen over the diagram, trying to remember the name of the trachea so he could label it.

"That is a strange dream," he assured her, his brow furrowed as he tried to talk and recall at the same time. "But most dreams are. I think you're right about the stress."

"You don't think the door is real?"

He chuckled. "I go to that comic section every week. I haven't seen any magical door or orbs or even people. People say that area is haunted, but not by flower doors."

"So there are rumors that it's haunted?"

Another shrug, followed by "Aha," and scribbling down the word lungs where the trachea was supposed to be. Kiera didn't correct him. She'd fix it later.

Once he was done and looking quite proud of himself, he glanced up again. "They just think it's haunted because it's dark and quiet. People just have overactive imaginations. I've been there countless times and never seen a thing."

Kiera nodded, conceding, and deciding he was right. It was silly to think the dream was real just because it was in a real location.

She didn't mention the dream again when they

finished class and went to lunch, where they met up with Tucker and Ezra. Once again, Ezra's skin was pale and almost turning grey. It reminded Kiera that her dream problems couldn't compare to Ezra's, so she kept her mouth shut and silently listened as

Tucker chatted about the folklore they were learning about in history class and how there could have been classes of magic that faded away or were forgotten.

Then, someone stepped up to their table and gently placed both palms on the edge, bringing attention to himself. Kiera turned quickly, as did Ezra, and just as she feared, Kent was looming over them. His eyes were wide, and his mouth turned upwards in an eerie, condescending smile that was probably meant to make him look like a kind, understanding professor but failed.

Ezra tensed, just like he always did, but didn't greet his sibling.

"Hello, little brother. Kiera." He nodded at her curtly, then, "Tucker."

Tucker muttered a quiet greeting, clearly uncomfortable.

Kent looked Ben over quickly, furrowed his brow, then ignored him. He must not have any classes with Ben in them, and Ezra probably never mentioned Ben's name to Kent. She wished *she* had the luxury of not hearing Kent say her name too.

"I just wanted to greet all my brother's best friends," Kent said. He took a moment to consider sitting down next to Ezra, then thought better of it and straightened. "And if any of you need any help with your studies, just let me know. I used to be a tutor during my university years. I have plenty of experience one on one."

Kiera didn't bother using tutors last year, and now there was zero chance of that, with Kent threatening to teach them.

"I know some of you will definitely need the help," Kent said, glancing over Kiera and making her stomach twist. He must know how poor her grades were at the start of last semester. Kent then turned to Ezra. "Especially Ezra. I understand why you were slacking off last semester, but there's no excuse now, so I hope to see you at the top of the class by the time spring rolls around. Wouldn't want to fall behind me, now would you? And I was a year younger in this grade too."

She was really coming to hate this guy. If she ever had a sibling, she would never treat them like this, especially when Ezra tried so hard to succeed in everything he did. "He spent most of the semester studying," she insisted, raising her chin at

Kent when he turned to her. "The only reason his grades dropped was that he was hunting a *literal* serial killer."

"Which nobody asked him to do," Kent countered. "It wasn't his job."

Heat raced up her neck, and she stood. "He was trying to save Tucker—"

"Kiera," Ezra interrupted, his eyes dead and voice monotone. "Leave it." He lifted his half-empty tray of food and stood. "I have to get to class."

Kiera thought she saw Kent smirk, likely thinking he won this battle, and it only made her angrier. Ezra's eyes told her he was used to this, though, and didn't want her to get involved. Her insides begged her to counter him and give Kent a piece of her mind, but she knew doing so would only make things worse, so she did as she was told and sat down again.

"You should focus that energy on your studies instead," Kent jeered at Kiera, then turned and walked away.

"Hateful man," Kiera whispered. He had no idea how much energy she expelled just trying to read and memorize spells. She nearly became an insomniac doing it. Yet all he saw was a number on a page and assumed she was lazy.

"Agreed," Ben said once Kent was out of earshot. "Good thing he has no clue who I am. What's his problem anyway?" He directed this question at Tucker, who sighed.

"It's complicated."

They all waited with bated breath.

"Actually, it's not that complicated," Tucker amended as Kiera and Ben settled down to listen. Tucker paused to take a bite of his food—green beans in a strange, yellow sauce—then continued, "According to Ezra, Kent's always been a total prick. He was born that way and never grew out of it, regardless of how much schooling and success he got. That might have made it worse, actually. Stroked his ego. Anyway. Ezra and Kent are the only two necromancers in the family line. Kent was originally going to be the only one, but once it became clear how much of a jerk he was, their parents started to worry he might either let necromancy corrupt him or use it for evil. By the time they realized that, most of the other kids had already moved on to other career paths. So they placed all their hopes on the youngest who was still in high school."

"Ezra," Kiera whispered. Not only was having all the responsibility placed on you terrifying, but

Ezra also had someone above him who already did it all and might even view Ezra as competition.

"Kent doesn't know any of what I just told you, of course. Not that I know of, at least. He just thinks Ezra's following in his footsteps. So Kent's always nagging him and pushing him to see how far he can go before Ezra snaps and gives up. The path Kent is on and expects Ezra to go on is..." Tucker's voice trailed off as though he'd been about to say something he shouldn't have.

"Is what?" Kiera asked. What was he holding back?

"Well." Tucker scratched his head, chuckling nervously.

Lucky for him, the lunch bell went off to signal that it was time to get to class, so before Kiera could dig any deeper, Tucker packed up and left with little more than a goodbye, and Ben headed off too, largely unbothered by all of this while Kiera was even more confused.

What path was Kent on that he wants Ezra to go on? And why did Tucker clam up?

❧　9　❧

The next couple of weeks were tough to get through.

First of all, Kiera kept dreaming about the golden door. Almost every night, she'd find herself in that library again, and it would get creepier each time. The shadows from the shelves were darker, there were fewer people, the silence was oppressive, and the orb moved faster when she followed it. All of this made the door seem to shine even brighter and stand out more. It was like a beacon, welcoming her into its embrace and begging her to open it so she could escape those dark spaces between the shelves.

But then she would wake up in her bed, shaking.

She used to have nightmares about the serial

killer last semester, but somehow this felt even worse. Maybe it was because that serial killer was no longer roaming free, and this door was a more recent thing. She couldn't put her finger on why the dream made her so uncomfortable. Perhaps the answer lay in her own mindset during the dreams. In them, she felt like a doll on strings, compelled to go against her own nature. She was both herself and watching her own body from afar, screaming at it not to touch the door because something felt wrong. But she also desperately wanted to see what it felt like and discover what lay beyond.

On Saturday morning, she awoke in a cold sweat and felt her clothes plastered to her body. As she rolled over so she could face the rest of her dorm room, her eyes immediately flitted to something bright and gold among the darkness.

It was the door, sitting right there in her room.

She gasped, shocked and confused, and then it was gone. It had been part of a waking dream, a hallucination.

For a moment, she just willed herself to take deep breaths. In and out. Then she turned on the light and scanned the room to make sure there was no illusive door of gold hidden somewhere in there. There wasn't. It was just her, her desk and chair, and a few piles of dirty clothes. One of the shirts had some white stains on it from when she tried to use a cleaning spell, and it failed miserably, bleaching the shirt instead.

It was seven in the morning. Kiera's head pounded as she reached for her phone and stared at it. This had been going on for two weeks now! She was frustrated! Why wouldn't it leave her alone?

She swore she wouldn't tell Ezra about this and worry him, but she didn't want to tell her parents since it might prompt them to drive all the way here. Ben didn't believe her, and she wasn't close enough to Tucker to confide in him.

So Ezra was all she had left. Besides, she hated keeping things from him. He had told her about his family, even though he liked to keep that part of himself hidden, so she shouldn't conceal things either.

Hey, she texted. He was probably still sleeping and wouldn't get this for another hour or two, but just sending a message should be enough to comfort her. *Had a bad dream.*

She was about to put the phone down and try to sleep again when her phone vibrated.

It was Ezra. *What happened?*

So he was awake. That or she woke him up, and he was sweet enough to answer right away. Her heart warmed as it often would at the smallest things he did.

She told him everything, even the parts she hadn't told Ben, like how scared she was and how her body felt like it had a will of its own. If this conversation had been in person, she might have cried. One dream on its own was fine, but the same one for two weeks weighed on her.

In the end, he sent her a silly emoji of a cat patting her on the head and assured her everything would be okay.

I've heard sometimes people exposed to too much magic get messed up dreams as a result. Your dorm neighbors might be practicing spells at night and it might be affecting you, he texted, and it made sense.

For two weeks, though? Kiera asked.

You studied for longer than that, he reminded her. *Why don't we go to the library together today and try to think of a solution? I want to see you anyway.*

There he was, distracting her with his words that could either be romantic or oblivious. Either way, it filled her chest with an addictive warmth, and she wished she could go to the library right now. Sadly, it didn't open until ten on Saturdays.

Sounds good, she said. Thankfully, he couldn't see her blush over text.

Maybe it'll put your mind at ease to see the library IRL, Ezra added.

Maybe.

Honestly, she'd avoided the library because she feared that same sense of being dragged around from her dreams. Plus, what if the door *was* there? She hated the thought of it.

Apparently, this weekend marked some kind of magic-wielder's holiday. Kiera had completely forgotten about holidays at all, so when she walked into the cafeteria to gobble down a quick breakfast, she was surprised to find little dragons the size of cats sitting on one of the counters where food was normally served. Some of the chefs were standing behind them, wearing black pieces of armor over their chests—presumably to defend against dragon fire.

In front of each dragon, of which there were five, were large bowls with what looked like cheese on the inside. To explain this, hanging above the counter was a banner marked "Happy Evocation Day." Evocation was the name for a class of magic that focused on elemental effects. Acid, cold, flame, and lightning were the most prominent ones, which explained why there were little dragons here today.

Under the holiday title were the words "Today Only: Dragon-Grilled Breakfast Burgers and Paninis." As soon as she read it, one of the dragons gave out a little puff of smoke and lit the bowl of meat and cheese on fire. The chef nearby used a wind spell to put it out quickly.

"Dinner and a show," she muttered. She might have enjoyed it more if she wasn't so tired from all her nightmares.

Unfortunately, although the presentation was excellent, the food didn't taste particularly amazing, so she just ate it as quickly as possible and headed to the library immediately after. She was eager to see Ezra again. They rarely met outside lunch and class now.

The festivities continued as she went, though. Inside the library was another event—this one was called "The Battle of the Elements." There was a small group standing near the door, and Kiera walked in just in time to hear the librarian explain the rules. This battle was composed of people trying to create an element with natural objects, like making acid with foods. Whoever could do it went onto the second round, where they would then try to cast the spell of that element as fast as they could.

It seemed a little silly in Kiera's opinion, but some people were clearly taking it very seriously. There were several tables prepared. One had a variety of ingredients, ranging from the aforementioned lemons and tomatoes to things like dragon spit and toad eyes. There were even a few old magical creature items, like orc toenails and goblin teeth. Those caught Kiera's eye more than anything since they were hard to procure and even harder to use in spells. Most magical creatures of the past had been deemed too dangerous for humanity and were banished, locked up, or relocated to places where humans wouldn't stumble across them. For that reason, she rarely got to see these items up close.

However, she couldn't get near the table, as next to it was another table filled with bowls as large as woks. These would be used to mix ingredients and cast spells. If Kiera got in the way of those spell components, she'd interfere with the contest.

So, feeling a little regretful that she hadn't taken a closer look first, she headed away from the spectacle and toward her favorite corner. She didn't want to get caught in a lightning bolt or acid blast anyway.

Then she swerved around a corner bookshelf

and saw Ezra sitting in the less comfortable of the two chairs there, and all thought of orc nails disappeared. He looked good today. He'd combed his hair, and there was some pink back in his cheeks. The darkness under his eyes was still present, but the skin around them crinkled as he smiled at her, so the raccoon eyes nearly disappeared.

"Hey," he said softly and stood before she could sit down. "I was worried they might start blowing stuff up over there before you could get through." He nodded at the event, and Kiera chuckled.

"Nearly," she said and took a seat. He did the same a second later. "You don't want to participate?"

"Nah." Ezra held up a necromancy book about morgues and preserving bodies. "I have to keep up with my studies." The words were sharp. He clearly didn't think he needed to study this much and was just doing it to meet Kent's demands. "But now that you're here, you take priority."

Do not blush, she warned herself.

"So, do you want to study first or keep talking about your dreams?" he asked.

"Well..." She took a moment to think about it. As she did so, he placed his hand over hers and intertwined their fingers. He'd done it so slowly that it caught her off-guard, and she lost her train of thought for a moment, then, "Let's study for a little while, at least until they're done with their event." But it might be nice to explore the library now, while the loud voices were still present. It would make this building feel less like the silent, oppressive library in her dream. "Maybe we should go now."

"Sure. I'm fine either way." Ezra shrugged, his nonchalance filling her with relief. He wasn't tensing up as he did during class.

As they got up and weaved around the event to the stacks, a part of her felt pulled forward. She wanted to explore the stacks. She had to find the door! It was so close. In her dreams, she could never get it open, but this was real life! She could finally see what was inside—

Kiera gasped and ground to a halt. She'd been moving much too quickly and even managed to outpace Ezra. What was that? Her mind had run away with her, just like it did in the dream.

"Am I dreaming right now?" she whispered to Ezra as he caught up with her.

"No. Why?" He studied her eyes. "Do you not feel well?"

"No, I..." She rubbed her forehead, trying to get the creepy thoughts out of her head. "I lost myself for a second there, that's all."

Now he was stiff again, concerned for her safety. "Should we leave?"

No! We're so close!

"No, it's okay. It's best to confirm that the door's not here like we said we would. If I see the wall is empty, hopefully then the dreams will stop."

"Right." Ezra nodded, convinced even though she wasn't. "Then let's go check."

❧ I I ❧

hankfully, as they walked hand-in-hand along the wall where the door should hypothetically be, it wasn't as dark as her dreams. The event going on behind them also created enough noise—with laughs, taunts, and cheers—to take away the creepy aspect. The only thing that made Kiera jump were spells creating the occasional boom of magical lightning and thunder.

That noise did dull the further away they got. After about a minute of walking, Ezra made a comment.

"This building's a lot bigger on the inside than it looks on the outside," he said. "How far do the stacks go?"

"For a few more minutes of walking," Kiera

replied. "It's hard to imagine Ben doing all this walking just to reach the comics."

"Yeah..." Ezra peered up at the ceiling and the windows, which weren't allowing much light to stream in because of the trees surrounding the building casting shadows. "Something seems a little off."

His statement made the hairs rise on the back of her neck. Was her dream right after all? Was there something cursed in here?

She shouldn't be worried. In one more minute, they'd pass the wall where the door should be, see nothing, and confirm that it was all just her mind playing tricks on her.

"It didn't look like this last semester," Ezra added. He would know. While Kiera spent all of last semester in her secret corner, he would go everywhere to find books on every subject. "The remodel must have made it bigger somehow. I'm curious what kind of magic they used."

Yes. That made sense. It was just the remodel. Maybe the staff wanted to fit more books and used some type of space-related spell.

Ezra kept peering at the ceiling and bookshelves, counting down some numbers she couldn't make sense of as they walked. Kiera, on the other hand, kept her eyes right on the wall. She could feel an itch on the back of her neck now. With each passing step, it got stronger and made her feel numb.

See? Nothing. Now they could—

Wait.

The somewhat dark area around them slowly filled with a golden glow, like there were trails of good just flitting around the air. It was similar to cartoons where a character can see the smell of something drifting through the air.

Then, a few steps more and past a particularly tall bookshelf, they found it.

Right where her dream always placed it was the golden door. It was faded, and the plants curving in and out of its surface were dead, just like in the dream. There was something downright sad about it since Kiera had seen it looking bright, full of life, and shimmering. Before, it had looked alive and enchanting. Now it looked pitiful and desperate for what it once had.

She wanted to bring it back to life again.

"I can't believe it," Ezra whispered, gulping and gripping her hand tighter. "It's really here. Your dreams actually were real." He paused to think. Meanwhile, Kiera kept staring at it. The itch was stronger than ever now, nearly putting weight on the back of her neck and prodding her to move forward.

"Are you sure you didn't see it before in real life?" he asked. "Maybe that's why you kept dreaming about it."

That would make sense, but she was sure she'd been asleep every time. "Maybe I was sleepwalking?" she ventured, though she didn't believe it herself.

She only took her eyes off the door for a moment to look for the little wispy orb. It was nowhere to be seen.

"Are you okay?" he asked, turning toward Kiera. "You've been silent this whole time. Should we leave? Or maybe tell the librarian about it?"

"No." No. She wanted to touch it. She wanted to see it in its most beautiful, glorious form again.

Kiera clenched her fists as the urge grew even stronger. Why come all this way and just look at it? She knew, just like in her dream, that the question of what would happen if she touched it would forever haunt her if she did nothing.

"Kiera?" Ezra whispered as she took a step forward and raised her hand toward the door. "What are you doing?"

"I just want to feel it," she replied. "See if it feels the same as it did in my dream." She inched forward even more.

Ezra looked at her, then at the door, then quickly grabbed one of her hands and squeezed it like he always did. "Something feels wrong, Kiera. We shouldn't do anything without an adult to supervise."

"We are adults," Kiera whispered, feeling her head turn fuzzy. "We're eighteen."

"You know what I mean," he said, his voice strained. "Don't touch it."

For some reason, her brain told her to shout at him. He couldn't tell her what to do! She was her own person and could make her own decisions. Why was he treating her like a child?

Where were these angry thoughts coming from? She didn't feel that way toward Ezra.

But she really wanted to feel those ropes again, maybe even to pull on them. There could be something amazing behind that door, like a genie that could grant wishes or a portal into a world far better than their own.

She had to know.

So with her free hand, she leaped forward and grabbed the rope.

Just like in the dream, the door sprang to life. The dirt seemed to jump right off the door, letting it shine and nearly blind Kiera with its color. The plants regained their greens and rainbow hues. They even started moving, shifting their leaves and pedals upwards like they were reaching for the sun. Kiera also thought she could see the white orb out of the corner of her eye for a moment.

At the same time, as Ezra gripped her hand too tightly from the suddenness of everything, she felt something else happen inside her. It was like her life was being drained from her, making her weak at the knees and forming a splitting headache. She felt some part of her leave that she didn't even know she had, like when you know you've forgotten something but can't remember what.

Ezra yanked her back, away from the door, and the feeling of dread and emptiness left her stomach as her fingers lost contact with the rope handles. However, she still felt like something inside of her was missing.

"We need to tell the librarian," Ezra insisted, making it an order this time. "And maybe the headmaster too."

Kiera knew he wouldn't consider telling his uncle about this unless it was really serious.

"I'm sorry," she whispered. "I... my mind was so fuzzy, and it felt like I was sleepwalking." It was like she had watched her body move without her consent, just like in her dream.

"We need to go," Ezra insisted, shaking his head and tugging her back the way they'd come, away from the door.

She made a move to follow him, more than ready to get away from the door now that she knew it had taken something from her.

But then they both froze as they heard a slight creaking sound behind them. The dread returned, filling the pit of her stomach with lead.

The pair turned with wide eyes. Kiera was holding her breath. It felt like someone or something was watching them, so they had to look.

The door she had never been able to open in her dreams before waking up had swung open on its own. Through it, Kiera could see a beautiful white glow, like the sun but otherworldly, and the sweet smell of flowers beckoned them.

Once again, that tug in the back of her neck and in her head now urged her forward. She had to see what was inside. If they told the headmaster, the professors would surely lock it up and she'd never know what lay beyond the door.

She turned to Ezra and saw him struggling too. Then he took one step forward. He felt the same tug now.

They had to see just once.

"We shouldn't do this," Ezra whispered, but his own voice made it clear he was having second thoughts.

"You feel the same way I just did... don't you?" Kiera whispered, begging him to be the same as her. She didn't want to be the only one losing her mind.

"Yeah, I... I do." He raised his leg, scrunching up his face in a clear effort to step back and continue toward the librarian, but he instead stepped forward, closer to the ominous and beautiful door. It was clear by the surprise on his face that he hadn't expected his body to disobey him. However, another part of him looked relieved that he'd gone forward.

This really felt like a dream.

Kiera pinched herself to make sure she wasn't sleeping, then stepped forward. She never let go of Ezra's hand.

"We'll just peek inside and then leave," she assured him, hoping that would be enough to satisfy this dumb pull on her mind. "Just looking can't hurt." But touching the door did. Why did she think going inside would be any different?

The true answer was she knew something about this was very, very wrong.

She just didn't want to think about that. It felt so much better and more satisfying to follow this other voice demanding she give in to her urges.

Besides, it was just a harmless little door. What could a door do to her, really, other than maybe slam shut on her? There was zero danger here. None. Zilch. Nada.

Kiera took the first step inside the door. Normally Ezra would have been the one to make the first move. He was protective of others, so putting himself in danger was like second nature to him, from Kiera's experience with the serial killer discoveries last semester.

However, in this situation, Kiera was the one with experience, and he was the one resisting. So, it only made that sense that she made the first move today.

First, she peeked through the door, and the sight beyond it was better than anything she had imagined from the unsatisfying dreams.

Inside the door, where a normal door would have led into the regular forest with a paved path for students to traverse, she instead saw a beautiful forest grove. The trees above were so tall and thick that they nearly blocked out the sun, so she could only see a glow from above with no obvious star emitting it.

The ground was only made up of short grass but to make up for the lack of flowers and bushes were small lights that hovered a few feet above the ground. They were a variety of colors, like pale pastels, but the most prominent shades were yellow and white. The orb that had led her here must be one of them.

She was immediately struck with a calming sense of familiarity. She'd followed the orb for two weeks, and now she'd finally found its resting place.

"It's safe," she assured Ezra and stepped through. She wanted to reach the orbs again. Doing so felt like hugging an old friend you hadn't seen for a while.

Ezra looked hesitant, with one foot still in the

library and one hand on the bookshelf nailed into the wall. However, it was clear by the light in his eyes that he wanted to enter, so he eventually did with a bit more prodding from Kiera.

However, despite following her in, Ezra's grip on her still remained as strong as ever, and as they both walked on the grass, he spoke again in a quiet hiss.

"We should leave," she said, struggling to force the words out. "Something's wrong, and you know it."

"We're just looking," she assured him, her head hazy and her eyes drawn to the wisps. "No harm in... looking." She felt like she needed to sit down from how woozy her mind was becoming.

After watching the lights flit about like fireflies, she reached out to touch one, and Ezra yanked her hand back to stop her.

"Just looking," he repeated her words. "Don't touch anything."

"Right." She nodded, but her heart wasn't in it. She felt sleepy now. So tired and at peace.

No!

She clenched her fists, squeezing Ezra's hand so tight he yelped slightly, and she took a step back toward the door. Ezra was right. They should leave.

She kept digging her fingernails into her palm, willing herself to keep a clear head.

There was no denying that this strange forest, which seemed to have no end, was intensely calming. However, there was something about the lights floating around them in a circle that sent a shiver down her spine. The faster they moved, the stronger the sensation became of being surrounded by death. For a split second, she could almost see teeth on the little things. Mouths opening to gobble them up.

"You're right," she whispered, keeping her voice as low as possible lest something unwanted hear them. "We should go." And shut the door behind them.

Whatever had infected her mind and forced her in here couldn't have good intentions. This entire place smelled like a trap. If she did take a nap like she wanted to a moment ago, there was zero doubt she would have been eaten or tortured or worse.

Ezra nodded, biting his lip for the same reason Kiera was drawing blood from her palms. Then they both turned back to the door and prepared to make a run for it past the little orbs.

Just as they took a step forward, a voice called out behind them, and it stopped them in their tracks.

$\mathfrak{F}$ 13 $\mathfrak{F}$

Standing behind them, right in the middle of
the circling orbs, was a small creature no
bigger than Kiera's head. It was a female,
with skin so pale it was snow white, and it glittered
like diamonds covered its entire surface. She had
long, flowing white hair to match, and her *clothes*
consisted of the vines, flowers, and leaves that
wrapped around the door. That was strange
enough, but what stood out the most, of course,
were the two sky blue wings protruding from her
back. They were the reason she was hovering in the
air, on the same level as the orbs.

It was a real fairy.

Kiera thought back to the orcs and goblins of
old, which had been locked up centuries ago and
banished. Fairies were in the same category. Most

of them were known for going extinct, and the rest were said to have left Earth for other realms. Kiera had never expected to encounter one in real life before.

The fairy raised her small hand and beckoned them closer. Her expression was a mix of both concern and friendliness like she was desperate for a friend. If Kiera wasn't so on edge, she might have listened. There was something disarming and sympathetic about the fairy's face. She looked like a cross between a child and teenager, with the vulnerability of both stages in life etched into her facial features.

"I'm sorry," she said immediately, her voice singsong but not matching her disarmed and almost fearful expression. "I know you want to leave, so before you go, I just have a request."

Kiera hesitated and ignored Ezra's tugging on her arm.

That curiosity was taking over again, controlling her.

"I need your help," the fairy said. "Please."

Kiera became all fuzzy again and could see Ezra feeling it, too, since his face was getting all wrinkled from resisting it. Their legs felt rooted in place like they were becoming the tall trees surrounding them. The wisps had also moved their circle, so Kiera, Ezra, and the fairy were in the middle of it.

"Run," Ezra whispered, his voice breathless.

Kiera nodded and tried to move but felt her ankle twist painfully. It took all her remaining strength to prevent herself from tripping entirely.

"Please don't go," the fairy implored. "Please."

This time, though, her voice was no longer that of a frightened, innocent child. It had grown deeper halfway through the sentence, transitioning to an adult woman's, then deepening into something one would only hear with a computerized voice changer. It rumbled in Kiera's chest, and she tried yet again to run as the fairy moved toward her. Why wouldn't her stupid legs move properly? They should never have come to this cursed place.

The fairy's face morphed along with its voice.

The pretty blue eyes shifted. The long eyelashes grew, stretching down until they wrapped around the eyes entirely, turning them into black holes full of string that spun around like a bowl of writhing worms.

The thing's perfect teeth grew along with the eyelashes, becoming long and then sharpening into needles that protruded from the darkening lips. A dark liquid began to seep from the mouth, landing on the perfect grass and making it shrivel up and turn brown. That death began to spread, eating up all the green in the grass and eventually climbing up the trees too, turning the brown bark black and making it shrivel up and fall right off the wood a moment later.

"Please," the fairy repeated. Her green outfit of plants dried up and fell off, revealing featureless skin beneath that looked more like desiccated desert ground that had just lost its water. The skin had cracks all along it, with black oozing from them.

Needless to say, all of this was enough to terrify both Kiera and Ezra. They didn't even need to bite their lips to sober themselves up. This was more than enough.

Kiera shook her head to rid herself of the final bit of wooziness, then both she and Ezra charged toward the door. They could already see it inching closed with a loud creak, trying to lock them in.

Ezra leaped through first, then turned and reached for her to pull her through. He used his other hand to hold the door open. As he touched its surface, he paled. It must be stealing the same thing from him that it did from her.

Kiera kept moving, finding it easier to run the longer she resisted the fairy's pull. She could hear more fairy voices behind her, begging her to stay, and judging by Ezra's horrified expression, there were more of them. She could feel more than hear them right on her heels, like wasps coming in for the kill.

"I've got you!" Ezra shouted and grabbed her arm. She felt him yank her shoulder so hard it nearly dislocated but didn't mind, as the fairy's voices were right against her ears now. Their voices bounced around in her head, deafening all other sounds.

Then her feet were on solid ground again, the voices faded, and she turned just in time to see Ezra slam the door on the approaching fairies. Kiera probably had two more seconds before they reached her.

Worried the things might try to force their way into the library, she pressed herself up against the door like a barricade, just as Ezra was doing. They both waited, panting, for something to happen. Then, when nothing did, they finally stepped away. The sense of being drained stopped, and Kiera could finally take a deep breath.

"What was that?" she gasped, her chest seizing from all the stress.

"Fairies," Ezra stated the obvious, looking perplexed. "They're supposed to be extinct."

"More importantly, why are they in our library?" Kiera added, perplexed.

They both stopped speaking for a moment, enjoying the silence, then Kiera realized something was wrong with that too. Why was it so quiet? Where were all the students participating in the event?

She looked around and couldn't even see any lights aside from the emergency ones. There wasn't anyone around either that she could see.

What was going on?

14

"We need to get out of here," Kiera said as Ezra grabbed one of the smaller bookshelves nearby and started dragging it toward the fairy door, which was still glowing, though a little less so now that they weren't touching it. "What are you doing?"

"Barricade," he said. "I don't want to risk those things getting out."

Kiera studied the door. It did swing outwards, so Ezra had the right idea. "I'll help."

After about a minute of pushing, since the bookshelf was heavier than it looked, they had the door covered. Then, they sprinted away from it and headed for the front door. As they ran, Kiera's fears were confirmed. There was absolutely no one here. The outside was also dark.

"What time was it when we got here?" she asked, wanting to hold Ezra's hand again for assurance but knowing they were running too fast for it to be practical.

"Ten thirty," Ezra said. He pulled out his phone and checked the time, then groaned. "It's one in the morning."

"How is that possible? We were only in that place for ten minutes, tops."

"I don't know." Ezra shook his head, then stopped talking as they reached the door. Thankfully, it opened from the inside, and they were able to escape into the fresh air. There were streetlamps along the walkways here. They didn't need to worry about wandering around in the dark with the threat of fairies hunting them.

"I'll walk you to your dorm," Ezra said. "Then I'll..." He sighed, clearly dreading this next part. "I'll wake up my uncle and tell him what's happened. I'm sure they'll put a stop to whatever this situation is."

Kiera was tempted to say, "Like they did with the serial killer?" but kept her mouth shut. This was the smart thing to do. Even though the authorities hadn't managed to stop the killer last time, hopefully this time, they knew what they were doing.

Then again...

"Do you think their renovations are what created the door?" she asked. "Or someone placed it there?"

"I don't know. My uncle wouldn't willingly place killer fairies inside his own school, though." Ezra shook his head. "It wouldn't make sense. He cares about the school's reputation more than anything. He'd never allow such a thing to happen on his watch."

"Then maybe it was an accident," Kiera said. She noted how his uncle cared more about the reputation than the safety of the students. Maybe she was just being negative because all she heard about his family was the awful things they did. Plus, Kent's presence didn't help.

"Regardless, I'll take care of this," Ezra assured her as they reached her dorm building and stopped at the front door. "Will you be okay by yourself?"

The thought of going to sleep and dreaming about that door again scared her, but she forced a smile and nodded. There was no sense whining about dreams when Ezra needed to focus on dealing with the real issue. "I'll be fine." She looked over his shoulder at the walk he'd need to take to reach the staff building. The lamps only did so much to light the way. "Should I come with you?"

He shook his head, raised his hand, and snapped

his fingers, creating a small ball of fire to rest in his hand and illuminate all twenty feet around him. "I'll be fine. I'm more worried about you."

He must be worried about the now obvious pull they both felt toward the door. "Don't worry. I won't be making the same mistake again. The faces of those fairies are embedded in my mind now." And would surely give plenty of nightmares in the nights to come.

Ezra looked unsure, but there was nothing either of them could do, so he headed off after giving her a tight hug that lasted a little longer than necessary. Then, she headed back upstairs and made sure to lock both her room door and the window. If an orb came near her again, she'd be sure to smack it with something.

❧

HER DREAMS THAT NIGHT STARTED WITH A recounting of everything that had happened. First, she was alone looking for comics, following the wisp, then touching the door. Then, she was suddenly with Ezra coming from the other end of the library and actually reentering the door. The fairy begged for help like last time, then tried to snag her as she and Ezra ran away. Everything was exactly the same, recalled with perfect detail and just as much terror as before. Kiera was sure her heart would give out from all the overworking it was doing.

Then, after all that had happened, she found herself alone in the library again. Ezra was gone. The orb wisp was gone. It was just her, in an unnaturally dark library, with the shining door beckoning her. The fairies' voices were in her head again, whispering her name in a sing-song manner with deliciously soft and sweet voices.

"Kieraaaaaaaaa."

"There's more inside to see."

"Don't you want to learn why we're here?"

"I know you're curious."

"Fairies can grant wishes."

"What's your greatest wish?"

Then they started listing off wishes all at once, their voices coming together in such a loud, head aching way that she screamed.

"Money. Gold. Love. Beauty. Brains. Magic. Secrets. Flight."

Then she heard, amongst all the superficial wishes, that first fairy voice saying things more in line with Kiera's actual thoughts.

"A life with Ezra. Your parents to remarry. Becoming a doctor. I can do those things for you.

All I ask in return is a little magic to make it happen."

Suddenly, she found herself in front of the door. It was like she had teleported forward without the use of a spell.

Then her hand was on the knob, tugging it open but feeling resistance.

Wait. The door had handles of rope on it. Why was she feeling metal?

Kiera gasped and opened her eyes for real this time. The fairy voices vanished, leaving behind only a faint echo that faded as well.

She was in her dorm room, standing up, and her hand was on the doorknob, tugging on it and trying to open the locked door.

"No!" She shrieked and fell backward. She'd been sleepwalking, probably heading back to the library to open that door again. If the door wasn't locked, would she have done it?

"This can't be happening," she whispered, scooting backward until the wall was behind her. Those things were controlling her in real life now, not just in sleep. They were using her body like she was a puppet.

She spent a few minutes muttering protection spells, trying to think of anything that would protect her mind. Unfortunately, necromancy didn't focus on protection. It was offense based, and most of it included spells used on those who were already dead or were about to be. She didn't want to be either of those things.

After casting a few shields that would shimmer in the light and hopefully save her from fairy dreams, she crawled back into bed. The clock on her desk said 4:15 AM.

Ezra had told his uncle, so there were probably magic-wielders poring over the door right now. Even if she did walk over there in her sleep, they would assuredly stop her. There was nothing to worry about.

She still uttered a spell that would potentially take away her dreams. She'd never been more tired but also more afraid of resting.

❧ 15 ❧

The spell must have worked. When Kiera woke up to the sun streaming right into her eyes, she couldn't recall any dreams. It had also caused her to oversleep, as when she looked at the clock this time, it read 11:14 AM. Breakfast would almost be over.

"Shoot." She leaped out of bed and looked down at her clothes. Her pants had a few grass stains on the bottom, and her shirt stank of sweat, understandably.

Her body still aching from yesterday, she changed into a fresh outfit, sprayed her hair with dry shampoo, and headed out the door. She was famished from not eating since yesterday morning and also wanted to see if anything had changed. As she headed out, she texted both Ben and Ezra to figure out where they were. Both of them answered that they were in the cafeteria and were wondering why she wasn't there yet. Ben's text was more of a joking demand, while Ezra's sounded genuinely concerned. She hoped he'd have good news to give her when she arrived.

The cafeteria was unusually crowded today. Gone were the dragons and holiday traditions. Instead, people had filled every spare seat, and nearly all the students were leaning forward, speaking in rushed, loud, excited tones. It gave Kiera an eerie sense of déjà vu since people acted similarly when the serial killer's first victim was discovered. Would their excitement turn to dread as it did back then?

She hurried to grab some food from the buffet, settling on quail eggs, goat meat which had been turned into bacon using magic, and some fruits she couldn't identify. They were either magically grown or an ancient type of food that wasn't grown outside of magic areas.

Then, it was easy enough to find Ezra, Ben, and Tucker seated at a small table in the corner. There were a few girls seated there as well—probably friends of Tucker—and all of them were in a heated discussion as well. The rush of words didn't stop as she took a seat and took a bite of a purple fruit that tasted like a sour apple.

"My u— the headmaster assured me the door would be locked up, and that section of the library closed off," Ezra was saying, catching himself before calling the headmaster his uncle. He looked up at Kiera as she sat down and flashed a smile that said he was happy to see her. "As long as we stay away from the area, we should be fine."

"Right." Tucker nodded. "We don't want a repeat of last semester." He nodded at Kiera, acknowledging her, before forking a hashbrown into his mouth. "The real question is, how'd the door get there in the first place?"

Kiera noticed Ben jump. His eyes darted across the table, as they often did when he had too many thoughts racing through his mind at once. Then he started spooning beans into his mouth so fast he nearly choked.

"You okay?" she whispered, making everyone turn toward him, including the two girls Kiera didn't know by name.

"Yeah, yeah." Ben's face assured her he wasn't okay, even though his voice sounded nonchalant. "Just some... research I did on the school last semester is coming back."

"Oh? Do tell," Tucker said. "Anything to unravel

this mystery." He glanced at the girls. "And reassure us that everyone's safe."

Ezra leaned forward, eager to hear. He didn't always take Ben seriously when they first met. Ben had a habit of joking about everything to avoid dealing with it, but Ben was so serious now that everyone was anticipating his next words.

"The campus has been here for a long time, right?" Ben began, putting down his fork so he could use his hands to emphasize each word. "With it comes a lot of ancient history. I've heard about a lot of stuff getting locked up in here, even back when this place was just a standard castle instead of a university."

Kiera knew about this, though she hadn't looked into it that hard. She'd been too focused on her own grades to care. Meanwhile, Ben's natural good grades must have given him enough time to read up on whatever he wanted.

"One of the tales that was spun about the place was a rumor about some fairies. Apparently, fairies used to live in these woods and torment the people here from time to time. They were often sent back into the woods, but no matter how many times the people living here fought back, the things would return after a couple of years.

"It wasn't until the place became a school that

someone actually did something about it. When the fairies started tormenting the students here—maybe even killing them, I don't know—the headmaster at that time worked together with other high-level magic-wielders and necromancers to be rid of the fairies once and for all."

"When was this?" Ezra asked.

"Maybe over a hundred years ago? The rumors couldn't be sure. They all passed down from word of mouth. Sounds like the headmaster tried to cover it up, so the school's reputation of safety remained intact."

"Some things never change," Kiera muttered, and Ezra nodded with a sarcastic chuckle. He knew that all too well.

"So, working together, the headmaster and all his buddies banished the fairies they couldn't kill to a small pocket realm where they wouldn't have access to anyone but themselves."

That sounded just like what they'd stumbled across. It was a small, self-contained grove that had the sense of being in a snow globe rather than part of a full, vibrant world. Those woods had both felt endless and contained like they only gave the illusion of distance. Who knows? Maybe the woods only went a hundred feet and just stopped.

"That would mean," Ezra said somberly, "That

the fairies are desperate to get out, just like we saw."

"Most likely." Ben picked up his fork again but just stared at it. Then he glanced at Kiera. "The book I read said the door was sealed with death magic. Does that mean anything to you necromancers?"

Kiera didn't quite understand the implications of that, but when she looked at Ezra, she could see acknowledgment in his darkening eyes.

"That's why the door looked the way it did," he said quietly. "All dried up and lifeless. But then we touched the door and—"

"But we shut it," Kiera cut in quickly, not wanting him to finish and confirm her fears. "We closed it and ensured it couldn't be opened again. Plus, I'm sure the professors have double locked it now, right?"

Tucker shrugged. "We can only hope."

"I'm guessing the door's always been there," Tucker continued quietly, as though continuing the story from before. "Even when we were here last semester." He shivered, likely recalling all his trips to the comic book section and how close he came to it. "The renovation must have accidentally taken away its concealment."

And Kiera was the one who answered its call.

Her stupidity could have doomed the entire school.

When she looked up, she saw Ezra staring at her and knew he could practically read her thoughts.

"It's a good thing we caught it when we did," he assured her. "Otherwise, someone else might have found it and went in alone. Then we would all be in trouble."

In translation, he was saying this wasn't her fault.

"Let's avoid the library today," Tucker finished, his voice loud enough to drown out their worried thoughts. "I say we all head to the recreation room and play some games or watch movies to relax." He directed this at the girls, who both looked nervous after the death fairies conversation. "It'll help to get our minds off things."

Kiera said sure, but she, Ezra, and Ben all had a look of fear in their eyes that couldn't be wiped out with a single game of table tennis. Until the professors confirmed that everything was perfectly safe, the threat still hung over them.

And the professors had lied to them before, claiming everything was fine when it wasn't.

Until they saw that door completely sealed or torn down with their own eyes, none of them would sleep well at night.

16

As much as she hated to admit it, playing a few games of table tennis and pool after Tucker's prodding eased her mind ever so slightly. It also helped that the windows in the recreation building offered a clear view of the library across the walkway and past the water fountain.

The interior of the recreation room was usually very crowded. There were three monitors with huge screens. Plugged in were three different game consoles, a DVD player, and dozens of movies deemed appropriate for their age group. There was also a spell listed on the wall that could make the images on the screens become three-dimensional if cast correctly.

On the other side of the room was the pool

table, two smaller tables for tennis, and a mini bowling alley that had to be enlarged with a spell before people could play it. Before doing so, one would have to move all three tables out of the way so the alley had space to fit. Then, when the person was done, they'd have to use the spells written on the walls to make it miniature again, so it was out of the way.

Since the recreational building was so close to the library, there were only three groups of people inside. The rest were as far away from the library as possible.

After playing a few games, Kiera sat down with Ezra on one of the couches near the window and settled in to watch Tucker and Ben face off against the two girls. Ben's nervousness was gone, replaced by a competitive attitude that had him insisting he switch teams so he could face off against Tucker. The girls were more than happy to do so to even things out. One of the girls had requested using a spell that would give her an athletic advantage, but the other three had shot that idea down in unison.

"I've been keeping an eye on the library," Ezra told her as she leaned against him. His head was angled toward the window, and his hands felt clammy in hers. "I saw a few professors leave, and some students enter, so it must be open for everyone." He clenched his teeth. "They should close the whole place off until it's completely safe."

"I agree." Kiera considered telling him about her sleepwalking, then decided not to. It would only worry him more. Besides, she planned to push her desk against the door from now on to prevent her from leaving the dorm. She wasn't taking any chances. Instead, she redirected the conversation to a different touchy subject. "How did your uncle *really* take the news about the fairy door?" she whispered.

Ezra pursed his lips in a way that made his cheeks bulge, then took a deep breath. "He wasn't the problem. He's proactive and focused on solving the issue quickly. It's my brother that's the problem."

"Kent? What did he do?"

"He shoved his nose into it, as he often does. He always thinks he has a say in things when he really doesn't."

"And... what did he say?"

"He said they should just wall off the stacks and leave it at that so there wouldn't be any liability. The school and family reputation are his priority."

Kiera squinted at Ezra, unsurprised. "But what if the fairies got out anyway? I don't think a wall could stop them."

"That's what I said. In all honesty, I think he was just saying that because I was there. If I wasn't present, I have a sneaking suspicion he would suggest keeping them here to study them. I'm sure having some magical killing machines would prove useful for his personal experiments."

"Does he... normally experiment on dangerous creatures?"

Ezra shrugged, looking a little sheepish. "Honestly, that was just a personal guess. There's no evidence that he does any of that. He just always seemed like the type." Ezra appeared lost in his own thoughts now. His eyes were staring forward and glazing over.

Kiera wanted to ask more. This was the first time he had spoken freely about his brother, but at that moment, she saw movement out of the corner of her eye. It was coming from the window.

"What's going on?" she whispered and pointed. The library door had slammed open, and students were pouring out of it, some with their mouths open. They must be screaming, though it was muffled through the glass windows.

A few seconds later, the librarian rushed out too and held the door open behind her. She was followed by two professors carrying a skinny young student in their arms.

Ezra saw what was happening and leaped to his feet, holding Kiera's hand. "We need to see what's going on," he said. Kiera completely agreed, and they ran out.

As soon as they opened the front door, the screams of the teenager being carried met their ears. He was shrieking at the top of his lungs in complete agony.

"Get them off me! Get them out of my head!"

17

Kiera followed behind Ezra, scanning the windows of the library for any flying creatures or little white orbs. She saw nothing. The only thing that still remained at the library was the librarian, who was guarding the front door with a spell book in her hand. She must be the last line of defense until other magic-wielders were called.

Then there was the student being carried about. Judging by his voice, he was pretty young—maybe sixteen or seventeen—but he was very tall. Despite being thin, he must have still weighed quite a bit. The two professors were struggling to carry him until one of them muttered a spell under their breath. Then, their arms relaxed, and they carried him easily. They were headed toward the staff area, where there was presumably a nurse's office. The boy would need medical attention. Whatever was making him scream had been brutal in its treatment of him.

His voice was hoarse as he continued screaming and thrashing against the two men carrying him. His eyes were also wide and bloodshot. They looked at Kiera once, though she could tell he was looking right through her, then he scanned the sky for any assailants.

The worst part of him was his skin, though. It was all red and fleshy. His arms, legs, neck, and the part of his stomach that was visible under his ripped shirt looked like someone had attacked it with a cheese grater. There were endless streaks across it, leaving some pieces of skin hanging right off, and it was all dripping with blood. There were also some spots on his arms that looked like they'd had chunked bitten out of them.

The thrashing couldn't be helping with those wounds. Luckily, Ezra also said a spell as the boy passed by, and it calmed the boy down enough to stop fighting the men trying to help him. The second professor shot Ezra an appreciative look then they continued forward.

"Stay away from the library," the librarian shouted at Ezra and Kiera, then at the others exiting the recreation building to see what was going on. "It's not safe. Head to the staff building. It has the most protection."

"I can help," Ezra said. "At least until backup arrives."

The librarian studied him, clearly recognizing him and the family he came from. Then she gave it a second thought and shook her head. "My priority is your protection—all of you. Go to the staff building, and if you see anything flying nearby, you run. Am I understood?" She had the authoritative voice of a military leader. It was so different from the soft, welcoming tone she used to greet incoming students on any other day.

"I should have known they wouldn't lock things up securely," Ezra muttered as Tucker and Ben joined them. "They never take anything I say seriously."

"Then if you think the authorities are failing again..." Ben lowered his voice as they all headed down the walkway as commanded, "Should we take matters into our own hands like we did last time?"

Kiera hated to disobey the *adults* but not doing so could result in more victims and zero solutions. "Maybe," she whispered. "But... surely the high-level magic-wielders can—"

"They have other priorities," Ezra cut in. "They

always do. That's why they're never around. There's always something big going on in some other state, so by the time they arrive, things have already escalated." He glanced at Tucker, who had been the last victim last time things got dangerous in the school.

"Then..." Kiera took a deep breath, knowing she was about to do the thing she always hated seeing characters do in books. They were about to go against the authorities even though they were unequipped. Well, Ezra and Ben were actually pretty advanced in magic, so at least they had some advantage.

"So, that's it then?" Tucker whispered as they reached the staff building. Other students were already huddled outside it, relaying what they'd seen to their friends. "We're going in? Should we go tonight or wait a few days?"

"We might not have a few days," Ezra insisted, looking more agitated by the second. "Yes. Let's go tonight."

Then it was settled. While Kiera didn't feel comfortable with the idea of taking on death fairies, she agreed with everything they said. Besides, she'd feel much better going with Ben and Tucker rather than just her and Ezra.

"All right." Tucker glanced at the two girls, who had been listening to their entire conversation and now looked unsure what to do. "Why don't you two stand guard for us?" he asked. "That way, neither of you are in any danger."

The girls hesitated, then nodded and started chatting with him about the best spells to use. Kiera still couldn't remember their names but their eagerness to help made her wish she'd bothered to ask a while ago. Once all this was over, hopefully she would get a chance to.

"That gives us ten hours to study spells that can be used against fairies," Ezra said. He was holding Kiera's hand again. They'd been doing a lot of that lately. Unfortunately, danger was so constant that Kiera barely had time to appreciate it. "We'd better get started."

18

Since the library was now off limits, Ezra told Kiera he'd decided it was best to study outside within eyesight of the building. That way, if something else suspicious happened, they would know about it. Ben decided to join him and Kiera while Tucker and his friends headed off to chat with some professors in an attempt to figure out any new information. Tucker also promised to ask what happened to the boy, though they already had a good guess. A normal animal wouldn't grind someone's skin up like that. It had to be the fairies.

Kiera and her friends weren't the only ones interested in the library. As they chose a bench in the garden near the library, surrounded by the fresh scent of spring air and moist earth, other students filled the other nearby benches too. Every single person sat facing the library. Some looked down at their phones or the books they'd brought with them, but there was no way to hide how often they kept glancing up at the place where a student had just been torn up.

"I heard this morning," Ben whispered to Ezra and Kiera, "That thanks to you two catching that serial killer, everyone's gotten a little braver and more proactive when it comes to mysteries around here."

"Oh?" Ezra frowned, not looking too pleased about that.

"They figured if someone like Kiera could figure out the answer to a mystery, they could too," Ben finished, probably unaware of his words being a veiled insult to Kiera. "So, we might not be the only ones trying to sneak in tonight."

"That's a good point," Ezra commented, studying the boys and girls sitting nearby.

Kiera heard one student whispering a spell that would let them see through some of the library walls, though judging by the student's sigh a moment later, there was some sort of barrier around the building that blocked magic sight.

"Hopefully, Sally and Meiying will be able to keep people out," Ezra finished, referring to Tucker's friends. Kiera immediately filed those names away in her head so she'd be able to address the girls later. She wondered if Sally might be the blond one who looked like she was always blushing, while Meiying was the dark-haired one who wore dark eyeliner and sported flowers on her clothes.

"I don't like getting more people involved when it's so dangerous," Ezra finished, "But I don't think we're dealing with just one person this time. We'll need the help."

Nothing happened for the next hour. The library doors remained shut, and the only person who went in the back was the librarian herself. She didn't stay in there for very long either.

Kiera practiced a few extra spells while they waited, focusing especially on flight, telekinesis, and death spells. The flight and telekinesis would hopefully help if the fairies flew out of reach. The spells for draining life were because if the necromancers who sealed the fairies used death magic, she would have to as well.

Her mind was starting to spin from all the reading, to the point where the straight lines on the page were curving, when Tucker and his friends arrived. Sally and Meiying. Right. She had to remember that now, though it was hard to recall both those names and the spells at the same time.

"So, we couldn't learn much," Tucker told the

group as they all sat down, some on the bench and others on the ground. "The kid was sent to the hospital and luckily only had skin-deep wounds that should heal. If the librarian hadn't found him when she did, he might have gotten a lot worse."

"So, what happened to him?" Kiera cut in, finding it hard to keep her voice low when they had so little time. "Did they find out what did it?" She already knew but wanted confirmation.

"The librarian found him in the back of the library, limp and wedged between some book-shelves. He didn't start moving until she touched him, and some other professors came to help. They didn't see what did it to him, only the result."

Ezra scrunched up his nose, unsurprised. "Well, we already know what did it. I just wish we knew more about stopping it." He put away the folklore book he'd been reading and motioned for everyone to get closer. They huddled up like a sports team about to decide their opening play. "We'll head through one of the back windows, going the old-fashioned way. I don't want to risk using a spell and setting off an alarm or wasting our energy before we really need it."

Kiera knew there were alarms set for magic more than for physical break-ins. Magic-wielders weren't worried about normal people breaking in. It was enemy magic users that were the real threat.

"Sally, you guard the back door. If anything seems amiss, use an alarm spell to let us know. If that doesn't work, just call on the phone. It's not as fast but should still work inside the library." He turned to Meiying. "I'll have you guard the front. Same deal. Warn us if something seems wrong and try to prevent other students from sneaking in. They don't know the real threat as we do."

"Actually, some of them do," Ben cut in, almost looking sheepish as Ezra turned on him. "I didn't want everyone to be in the dark. I don't want a repeat of last time, where it was just me and Kiera against a killer. So, I told some of my friends about the fairies, omitting the part about you guys releasing them."

Kiera squinted at him. "Seriously? You think we released them?"

"The renovation was what unearthed the door, in my opinion," Tucker offered. "You just... opened the door."

"Regardless of what brought them," Ezra said, his voice deepening in annoyance from their distraction. "We need to focus on the task at hand. We can point fingers later. I'm sure my uncle will do the same," he added grumpily, then drew a map of the library in the sand. "We'll go in through this window and keep it open behind us as an exit route."

"We should open a second window on our way there, just in case," Tucker recommended, making Ezra nod before continuing.

"Then we'll find the door and see what we're up against. I have some sealing spells available and know Ben has some too."

Ben nodded. He was the main magic-wielder in their group, after all.

"But I think the door and its relation to death, or rather the lack of life, is the key here," Ezra added. "When we found the door, everything on it was dead. It only opened after we touched it and something about our touch made it spring to life."

Kiera looked down, recalling exactly what happened. The flowers on the door had been completely lifeless. Then when she touched it, she felt like something was drained from her. It was like losing something inside her that she wasn't aware she had. Had it been draining her life or energy to wake itself up?

Ezra confirmed this a second later. "I suggest we use a spell to remove the life from the door as well. Kiera and I specialize in that as necromancers, and if we work together and suck away every ounce of energy from the door, it should close again. As far as Ben's research says, that's how the door works. The fairies need life to thrive and fly, so without it, they can't get through the door."

Ben looked a little unsure, especially when Ezra brought up Ben's research. "I could be wrong," he said quietly. His insecurity only popped up when it came to really important things like this. "I was just going off rumors most of the time."

"Well, it's all we've got." Ezra glared at the library and what lay within. "I don't expect my uncle or brother to do much about it today other than locking the place up until they spend several meetings debating what to do, and by that point, it might be too late."

"Or..." Tucker bit his lip. "What if our interference makes things worse? You two should have left the door alone the first time, and now someone's been hurt. What if—"

"We caused the problem," Kiera cut in. She could tell Ezra was getting agitated from the thought of his inactive family, so she spoke before he could say something harsh. "We opened the door, so we'll be the ones to close it. Besides, it's not like we're working alone like last time. We have Tucker now and Sally and Meiying. Plus, everyone's keeping an eye on the library, even the students. I don't think this is as risky as last time."

Ezra gave her an appreciative look, then started out handing out papers to everyone with spells written down in his small, neat handwriting. "So, let's review these spells one more time before we have dinner and prepare to break in."

"To think a relative of the headmaster is the one planning a break in," Ben joked as they all settled in to study.

Ezra just laughed good-naturedly before returning to his teaching mode. "Let's get started."

❦ 19 ❧

Sneaking into the library was as easy as Ezra made it sound during the briefing. There wasn't anyone watching the place, though the security cameras were all pointed at it, and it was easy enough to find the cameras' blind spots and slip around to the back. Meiying stayed near the front, resting on a bench in the shadows to keep an eye on the exterior of the building.

After they said goodbye to Sally at the back, Ben easily got the window open. It was a basic window one might see in a suburban home, though it was slightly taller than average. It also had a small, simple metal lock that just needed some prodding with a metal device Ben happened to be carrying.

"My favorite comic is Red Rogue, the Spy

Detective," Ben explained as he fiddled with the lock, making slight clinking and clacking sounds as he did so. "He says one should never go outside without a lockpick. You never know when you'll need it."

"Really?" Kiera crossed her arms and smirked. "How often do you need to break into things?"

"People lock themselves out of cars and houses all the time. You'd be surprised by how many people never keep spare keys too." He stopped talking for a second, focusing his full concentration on the lock. "Doesn't help that it's so dark," he whispered to himself.

"Do you need light?" Ezra offered his hand, in which he could create a ball of fire with one sentence.

Ben shook his head. "You'll need to save your magic for later," he whispered.

After another minute, in which the rest of them stood there awkwardly and wondered whether they should find another way in, there came a loud click, and Ben breathed an excited sigh.

"Got it. I knew I would," he said, his voice making it obvious he *didn't* really know if he would succeed or not. "Ladies first." He gestured to Ezra and Tucker, receiving an elbow in the side from Kiera instead before she pushed open the window and climbed in. She was terrified of going inside this place, but the need to put Ben in his place was stronger.

There were fewer lights on than before, though luckily, Tucker cast a spell on them earlier that improved their eyes ever so slightly to see in the dark. It wasn't much, but it was better than using a real light and revealing their position.

Once all four of them had climbed onto the floor as quietly as they could, their spell page from Ezra either in hand or tucked into their pockets, they headed toward the door.

Kiera made sure to circle around the door's location rather than walking straight toward it. She also kept an eye out for any of those wisps. They'd be the first sign of danger. They could be some sort of alarm-giving creature or security cameras. If she saw one, she planned to immediately use either a fire or death spell on it, depending on how many there were. If there was just one, she'd use death to end it quickly. If there were multiple, she'd use fire. It had a wider range. Death could only affect one target at a time, so while she focused on one, the others could get away.

She constantly felt Ezra at her back, and it brought her comfort. They'd made a good team before. Their different ways of using magic melded together well. Plus, unlike their last encounter with the fairies, they knew what to expect and had spells in mind. When one was caught off-guard, it was hard to think up magic without extensive practice in combat. Without that element of surprise, Kiera's head was clearer.

As they came closer, Kiera began to hear something. It was faint—almost so quiet that she told herself it was her imagination. She could hear the ever so slight sound of music coming from something that sounded like both a flute and a violin at once. It was emitting a cheerful sound, like flowers in bloom mixed with a singing brook. Hearing it in such a dark place where they could hear their own footsteps and the creak of the floorboards was unsettling.

"I hear music," Ezra whispered, confirming her fears. When she stopped and looked at the other boys, they had the same expression of fear and discomfort. None of them liked the sound of music because they knew who was playing it.

"It's coming from the door," Kiera whispered. The door, or at least its general direction. "At least we know where it'll be."

"Could be a trap," Tucker warned, scanning their surroundings for threats and finding none. "What should we do?"

"Proceed." Ezra rose slightly, sucking in a deep breath, then stepped ahead of Kiera protectively. He then headed forward, his spell page crumpled in his fist.

They got a little closer. The music got louder. A small voice singing in a foreign, ancient language joined in. It was feminine and beautiful—soothing like what one might imagine a siren sounding like.

The faint golden glow of the door became visible, too, casting an enchanting gold color on their faces. Kiera could feel that same sense of sleepy nonchalance overtake her again, but this time she was ready for it and cleared her head easily. She also held her fingernails closer to her palm, just in case she had to use pain to keep herself awake and alert.

Ben and Tucker had been warned of the effect the fairies had too, but when she glanced at them, she could see Ben's eyes drooping already. She hoped she wouldn't have to shove him out of the way to prevent him from giving in.

By the time they got within ten feet of the door, the music was at a regular volume. The voice was so clear it almost felt like it was inside Kiera's head.

Then, they stepped around a bookshelf, and their objective came into view. The music and singing stopped. The glow lessened. All that was before them now was the golden door and its green plants weaving around its surface. It wasn't particularly glowing or shining now. It just looked like a pretty, lifeless door.

It was also open a crack.

"I don't like this," Ben whispered, though he didn't suggest turning back.

There were the remains of yellow tape around the door, though some of it has disconnected from the surrounding wall and hangs awkwardly, clinging to the little connection it has left. There are also a few signs in front of it with the words WARNING: DANGER. That clearly wasn't enough to stop that one kid from taking a look, though.

"They should have just shut the whole building down from the start," Ezra muttered resentfully, then takes a step closer to the door. He's nine feet away now. "I'm going to shut it."

"Wait." Kiera grabbed his arm, shaking her head. Ezra, just like the rest of them, had fallen into the trap of forgetting magic when it came to simple tasks like shutting a door. Unless someone grew up using magic constantly, it was easy to become complacent and only recall magic's uses when it came to big things like healing gigantic wounds. "I can shut the door from here. Telekinesis."

"Right." He nodded, gulping nervously. "Sorry. Should have thought of that."

She patted his shoulder, not blaming him at all. They were all understandingly nervous.

Thanks to her previous practice, she recited the spell easily without missing a single word. Then she felt the magic move away from her, like a third arm stretching much farther than her real ones could. It felt flowy and liquid while at the same time solid and almost lucid.

Kiera forced it forward, concentrating on the edge of the door. Then, the "arm" pushed it shut as easily as any other door.

Once she heard a satisfying click, she withdrew her magic and ended the spell. The third arm moved back toward her, then vanished like a candle blown out.

Everyone waited for something to happen, which it did. A second after her spell ended, the door made a second clicking sound, and it swung a few inches open with a slight creak. Kiera felt like it was mocking her attempt with its whine.

"Great," Ben whispered, his voice shaking. Meanwhile, Tucker frowned at the entrance, arms crossed. Both of them were studying the door since this was their first time seeing it.

Kiera turned to Ezra, who was frowning and already muttering magical words under his breath.

"So," she whispered in his ear. "Death magic?" *Just like he said to do during their earlier plan?*

"Yup." He stepped back, so they were side-by-side again, and held up his paper for her to see, though she didn't need it. "We'll drain the door, and hopefully, that'll be enough for now."

"Wait." Tucker stepped closer. "Wouldn't the headmaster have already tried this? What if it fails?"

"I don't know if they tried anything," Ezra said, that bite entering his voice again. "Like I said earlier, they're probably waiting for backup first, but the time to act is now."

"But what if—"

"We won't know if it works until we try," Ezra finished. Once again, his shoulders were bunched up from nerves. "Kiera, are you ready?"

She hesitated for one second, glancing at Tucker, but knew Ezra was right. They didn't have much time, to her knowledge, and this was the best plan they could produce. Plus, they'd seen how responsible the authorities were in the past, or rather how irresponsible they were.

"Yes," she said, holding up her hands at the door. "Let's do it."

20

Kiera truly half expected the door to swing open and for fairies to charge out as soon as she and Ezra started to perform their magic. That was why she kept one leg behind her, bent, prepared to dash if they were attacked. Ben was the only one who had brought a weapon, and it was just a dinner knife from the cafeteria, which he kept in his pocket. Plus, who knew if physical weapons even worked on fairies? Did they? Would they? Most of the tales regarding the fae were old, outdated, and completely based on rumors that weren't true.

The only thing that brought her security was knowing that she had Ezra's presence at her side. She had no doubt he would do anything to protect her. His guard dog-like personality was endearing.

She just hoped that if things came to it, she'd be able to return it.

Tucker and Ben stood on either side of them as they began reciting the spell. Tucker even grabbed one of the heavier books off a nearby shelf to use as protection, though the spells he knew would probably be more useful. Kiera was sure the weight of a real object was just there for comfort. Old, normal human habits die hard.

Their chanting started off quiet and disjointed. Kiera had trouble aligning her words with Ezra's at first, making it sound silly. However, as she felt magic begin to move from her toward the door, her voice melded with his just as she felt his magic do the same. She was even able to stop focusing on the words as they repeated the lines a second time, then a third. Soon, it was like singing a song absent-mindedly while multitasking. It became effortless.

The door did nothing for a moment, not a single, solitary thing, giving the impression that the spell had no effect. Shortly, the green, blue, pink, and golden flowers began to wilt, then to turn brown. It was working. They were draining its life and hopefully locking the door once again.

But then, suddenly, the flowers sprang to life again, bigger and brighter than before. The glow they had seen when they had entered had returned, getting brighter and brighter until it was dazzling, almost blinding. There was also a faint buzzing sound, like that of an old television set. One from the middle of the twentieth century.

Kiera saw Ben glance at her out of the corner of her eye. Then he began reciting his own spell. She couldn't make out what he was saying.

"Keep going," Ezra told him, then continued the spell.

Kiera resumed, too, though seeing the flowers continue to bloom despite them clearly trying to kill them was unsettling. She also couldn't be sure, but was the door opening again? Just an extra inch? Could it be?

As the tree's exterior grew from all the rising greenery, she felt that same sense of loss that happened when she touched the door. This time, though, thanks to the sensation the spell brought, she knew what it was.

Normally, when she cast a spell, she could feel the magic leaving her as it went to create or interact with the spell she was commanding it to do. Then, the magic would come back to her.

This time, she could feel the magic leaving her, but it wasn't coming back. Instead, it was entering the door, either through the crack or into the flowers. She couldn't tell which.

"Ezra." She stopped chanting, feeling her legs weaken and her head dull. "Stop. We need to stop. It's taking our magic."

But Ezra didn't stop. He didn't even react. Could he not hear her?

Her vision was going fuzzy now too. The brightness of the door was making everything go white. Now she couldn't hear Ezra's chants. Had he stopped, or was she just going deaf?

There was the vague, nebulous sense of the ground coming closer to her, approaching, approaching, then all sensations stopped. She was merely existing in a world of complete whiteness, then blackness, then nothing. A void. A complete and total void. And she wasn't awake anymore, or maybe even alive.

She was nothing now.

She was no more. At all.

21

It took a few seconds to realize she was asleep, not dead, but those seconds felt like hours in her state. Luckily, once her out-of-it mind righted itself and understood that she'd fallen to the floor and become unconscious, she snapped out of her empty dream.

Her eyes were still closed, but she could feel the floor beneath her again. It wasn't solid wood, like the library, but uneven and earthy. She was lying on the ground outside. But how? Unless she was inside that fairy realm again, though that didn't make sense either. She was clearly lying on dirt. The inside of the fairy door was full of grass.

As she thought this through, she regained the use of her arms and legs. She moved one of her fingers, then scrunched up her toes in her boots.

Good. She was definitely not a corpse. Not a moment later, her eyes opened, and she blinked, in complete control again.

Above her were the long, stretching branches of tall trees. The bark-covered arms melded together, wrapping around each other to block out the sky. There was still enough light around her to see, but it wasn't coming from the sun.

She sat up. The light was coming from the small, glowing white orbs floating at various levels around her. They were bobbing up and down calmly, like buoys on the ocean, and weren't forming a perfect circle like last time. They were just existing now, going about as they pleased.

The lack of green around her became more apparent as Kiera looked around, searching for the door. The trees had no leaves now, and instead of grass, she was just sitting on deep brown dirt. The illusion of a beautiful forest full of energy and vibrance was gone. Now the forest's true form was shown. It was dead, and some of the trees were already dying. Their branches were drooped.

She could also tell now that this forest wasn't infinite. The trees seemed to stop at about a hundred feet, and beyond them was complete noth-ingness like her dream was a moment ago.

There were fairies too, but all of them had

shown themselves this time. There was no point pretending Kiera wasn't outnumbered.

The creatures were no longer wearing a glamour to make themselves pretty either. Their wings, which previously looked like they belonged to sparkling butterflies, were now ugly stick-like things that protruded from their bodies in odd ways like bones. Between the bones were black cobwebs, strung together so tight that Kiera almost didn't realize that's what they were.

Their faces were the same, with long sharp teeth and black eyes wrapped with that same black webbing. However, their skin looked worse than before. It was stretched in odd ways like there wasn't enough skin to cover their skinny bodies, and Kiera could see black and white flesh underneath at certain points the skin couldn't cover.

Everything about them was hideous and nightmare-inducing, including the stench of dead and rotting skin that emanated from them. There was also red blood on their teeth, even though their skin pretty clearly wouldn't bleed something that color. It must have been from that boy they nearly killed earlier today.

"Welcome back," the fairy whispered, her voice a mix between a snake and that beautiful siren song from before. "We missed you, Kiera."

Kiera couldn't be sure which of the fairies was speaking, as they all had their mouths open and were vibrating. It looked like any of them could be moving their mouth.

She glanced over her shoulder and finally found the door behind her. It looked the same here as it did on the other side, but all the leaves and flowers on this side were completely dead. It was also open slightly, just like before. The fairies must be afraid to let it close completely. That, or it was never meant to shut unless the entire thing was dead.

Speaking of that, how did the original magic-wielders close it the first time? If using death magic didn't work, how did they do it? It might be a spell long forgotten, or she and Ezra were just completely off the mark.

Regardless, failing with that meant she had no clue how to kill these things or lock them up. So, she might as well hear what they had to say.

This time, the voice of the fairy who spoke was familiar. It must be the one who greeted her the first time. Her singsong tone clashed with their surroundings.

"We understand your reaction to us," she said calmly, like a mother addressing a disobedient child. "And we're sorry if we've caused you any distress, but we can't allow you to shut the door."

Kiera was tempted to say *What do you want?* or *Why won't you just leave us alone?* but knew doing so wouldn't get her anywhere. It was clear the fairies only wanted to speak and weren't planning to answer questions.

There was a strong pulse in the air as the fairies moved slowly around her. It was like the entire grove had a heartbeat. It also rang inside her head, weakening her and making her stay seated on the ground rather than getting up.

"Our plan has never been to harm you or your kind," the fairy assured her. "We simply reacted out of necessity when you tried to lock us in again. We've been trapped in here for what feels like eons and know we will soon die if we do not get out."

That didn't sound like such a terrible thing after what they did to that student, but Kiera let them continue. She was now aware of something else around her own body, keeping her from completely sitting on the ground. It made her skin tingle and her hairs stand up. Was it a force field? She hadn't placed one around herself.

But maybe Ben did. That could have been the spell he was casting when she was busy with her own magic.

"Now that those monsters, those human men, are long dead, we can finally return to our home and live in peace once more," the fairy said, only allowing her calmness to fade when she spoke of the men who locked her up. "All we ask is one thing from you, one gift that will allow us to leave this prison, and then we will leave you and your fellow humans alone."

Kiera frowned, knowing she'd need to choose her words carefully. This protective shield on her wouldn't last forever and might be the only thing keeping these friends from attacking her as they did that boy.

"What is it you're asking for?" she asked slowly, enunciating each word and ensuring she didn't say her name or anything that might give them an edge. She'd heard fairies could use one's name against them.

"Oh." The fairy sounded shocked that Kiera would even consider agreeing, which she wasn't actually doing. She just hoped the answer would tell her how to defeat these things. "It's something small and simple. You won't even miss it."

"What. Is. It," Kiera repeated, not liking how twisty this thing's words were.

The fairy grinned, its gleaming teeth stretching fear beyond its lips. "Oh, I think you know, little dear."

Then, all the fairies sped toward her.

{A chapter ornament} 22 {A chapter ornament}

A lot of things happened at once.

Kiera scrambled to her feet, ignoring how the hard dirt ground scratched her knees and how tired it made her. Her entire body screamed, protesting as gravity pushed her down.

At the same time, the speaking fairy and all the others leaped toward her. Their mouths opened, and teeth moved forward, stretching like retractable cat claws. Kiera had barely taken one step toward the door when one of those jagged edges cut into her arm, digging in and not letting go.

She screamed as pain shot through her. She tried to run toward the door, but more and more teeth cut into her arms, hands, and legs. Then, when she tried to move, they tightened their grip.

She was only freed after the teeth let go, dragging along the skin and pulling it up like tractors pulling up farmland to get at the vegetables underneath. The pain was so searing and blinding that she nearly fell unconscious again. What made it even worse was that she could feel the magic being scraped off her just as quickly as flesh and blood. Now she understood why the boy looked like he'd been attacked by a cheese grater. All these fairies, holding onto her arms with their hands and digging in, had bitten off his magic and flesh alike.

"Ezra," she screamed and tried to continue toward the door but couldn't. Her shield from Ben was clearly gone now, and—

Wait, what was she doing? She could use magic! Just like before, she'd been so panicked she forgot to use a spell.

Maybe the death magic would work on the fairies, if not the door.

As the fairies shrieked with glee, making gobbling sounds as they tore at her, she focused on one of the fairies and hissed the words for the spell. The magic flowed from her like a river, then hit the fairy.

However, instead of draining its life and weakening it until it died, the fairy seemed to perk up. Its blackened eye sockets widened, and it released her just long enough to grin in her direction. "Very kind of you," it whispered, then grabbed Kiera's hand and dug its teeth right into her palm, harder than last time. The spell had strengthened the fairy rather than weakened it.

Kiera screamed again, the reality of her death hitting her fully, then she turned her words into a chant instead, forming the words for telekinesis. They were easier to remember seeing as she'd just used it a few minutes ago, and in a few more seconds, she gave a final shout and used her remaining magic to shove all the fairies away from her. The attack was weaker than she would have liked. She had significantly less magic to draw from, but it was enough to get their sharp teeth out of her. Unfortunately, some of her flesh went with them in jagged chunks, and she could already feel her blood dripping down her body and covering the dirt. Her already weak body was losing blood now too.

She used the last of her magic to shove herself forward and right toward the door. Sobbing from the pain, she pressed her arms against her head to defend herself from the blow, then hit the door with a thud. It swung open, and she felt herself hit a hard floor.

She was back in the library. Once she was down,

she felt the magic fizzle out completely rather than go back into her body. It was just... gone.

"Kiera!" Ben's voice rang in her ear, and she felt him yank her away from the door. Then she heard footsteps followed by the door closing. As she opened her eyes, she saw Ben standing over her, tugging her to her feet, and Tucker was weakly standing in front of the door, his back pressed against it to form his own barricade. A second later, there came a thump from the other side of the door. The fairies were trying to get out for good this time. Maybe stealing Kiera's magic had been enough to let them leave the barrier or whatever had held them back before. They didn't need to lure boys into the grove now. They could finally escape.

"Where's Ezra?" she asked, looking around weakly and willing her eyelids to stay up.

In answer to her question, she saw him lying unconscious on the floor beside her. The spell he cast with her knocked him out too.

She breathed a sigh of relief, grimacing when the faintest movement brought back more pain from all the bites and cuts on her body. Looking down, she could see wounds identical to that boy's. Luckily, none of the fairies had thought to bite her neck. She might have died completely if they did that. Maybe that was part of their plan, though. Perhaps they wanted to get all her magic before killing her.

"We need to go," she said, wanting her voice to sound loud and authoritative, but it came out weak and pathetic. "Now! We can't stop them."

Tucker and Ben didn't protest. She felt arms under her. A moment later, Ben was carrying her on his shoulder. Tucker did the same with Ezra. Then, they ran toward the front door, shouting for Sally to run away from the back and for Meiying to open the front door so they could get out. Luckily, she heard them, and when the door wouldn't open, she used a spell to break the glass on the front, leaving just enough room for all of them to escape.

Then, they were running down the walkway toward the staff building, where all the professors were sleeping. They'd need all the help they could get.

As they ran, they could hear giggling and singing, followed by what sounded like an explosion. Kiera could see beams of light stream through the windows, then the voices of the fairies spread throughout the building. They were out and hungry for more magic.

23

Everything was a blur as Ben carried Kiera down the path, the screeches of fairies trailing along behind them, though they were falling behind. Kiera had to blink several times to keep herself awake. Then she tried to remember a healing spell to use on herself. She could already hear Ben muttering something, which explained why the pain was slowly fading from her body, but she wanted to help.

However, as she finally recalled the right words and tried to whisper them, she felt nothing come from her body. There was no magic within her other than a small flicker that wasn't strong enough to do something like a healing spell.

"They took it," she said to Ben, agony ripping

through her as she realized she was defenseless. "My magic."

"I figured," Ben said before going back to his spell. He tightened his grip on her, which she was grateful for since she was having trouble keeping her head up. The only thing that helped her stay conscious was the loud screams of those monsters and the knowledge that the cries and giggles of glee were heading toward the dorms, where all the students were currently sleeping. In a few minutes, they'd be in the same state as Kiera was now, if not worse.

"I have to find Meiying," Sally said and veered away from Ben and Tucker. Kiera could hear her using a spell similar to Ben's magical barrier. Kiera hoped the girl knew what she was doing. She was too tired to warn the girl. Besides, what could she say? Be careful? Don't use spells on them? That wasn't super helpful.

Once they were past the dorms, Kiera knew they were nearing the staff building. She was facing backward, so she couldn't see it, but the glow of the lights inside the building was enough to assure her at least someone was awake.

She heard Ezra's voice then and was filled with relief that he'd woken up.

"Put me down and tell the nearest adult to

spread the word," Ezra said, his voice tired but carrying as much authority as he could muster. "I'll call my uncle and brother." There was no hesitation this time when referring to Kent. Desperate times called for desperate measures.

"Right," Tucker said, then opened a door. Kiera heard him stomp inside, then put something heavy on the ground. It must be Ezra. Then Kiera heard Tucker run off to warn people just like Ezra told him to.

A second later, she and Ben were past the doorway, too, and Ben was putting her down on the ground. Her legs were shaking but held her up again, and when she looked down at her arms, they were scarred, but the wounds had been sealed up. She would need an actual magical doctor to make sure there was no infection or damage, but for now, this was enough to stop the blood loss and block out the pain.

When she looked up and out of the doorway, her eyes cleared enough to see dozens of fairies streaming out of the broken glass windows in the library and speeding toward the dorms. Only one of them turned and came toward Kiera.

"Step back!" Ben shouted and grabbed the edge of the door. Kiera began a protection spell, but by the time she was through the first sentence, Ben had shut the door, and they heard the loud crash of the fairy running right into it.

"Don't worry," Ezra whispered from his spot on the ground, leaning against the hall wall and fiddling with his phone. "This building has shields around the exterior. Unless someone in here opens a door or window, it'll take a little while to get inside."

"Do the dorms have the same protection?" Kiera asked, recalling something about it in orientation but not recalling the specifics.

"Yes, but like I said, if a student hears what's going on and opens a door, the fairies have a way in." Ezra shook his head, pressed a button, then raised the phone to his ear. "Which we know means the fairies are probably inside already."

Kiera's stomach painfully flopped as she realized, once again, this was all her fault. They should have left well enough alone. First, she followed her dreams, which she knew were evil, and brought the door to life. Then, when the fairies were still trapped inside, she gave the fairies enough magic to drag her in and drain her of what was left.

Ezra didn't acknowledge any of this as he started speaking on the phone, his voice raised to a near shout.

"The fairies got out and are going to kill people

if you don't do something... That doesn't matter right now. What matters is that you protect everyone..." He clenched his fist and pressed it against the hardwood wall. "They drain magic, even when spells are used on them... If you knew that already, why didn't you say anything?" Another pause, in which he looked regretful or sheepish about something—probably their foolish actions. "I'm sorry," he finally said, which she'd never heard him say to family before. "We're inside the staff building, but the fairies are headed for the dorms. If you care about the school's reputation so much, protecting them should be your first priority." He did a final pause, then hung up without saying goodbye and looked up at Ben and Kiera.

"So, what's the verdict?" Ben asked, clearly not going to like what he was going to hear.

Ezra groaned, ran a hand over his face, then tried to pull himself to his feet. His legs were shaking too. "He's not even on campus, but he's on his way," he replied.

"And your brother?"

"They were together," Ezra said quietly. "They left to meet with relatives of the original owners who knew how to keep the fairies back."

So, Ezra had been wrong about them. They had been doing something to stop the fairies. Kiera and

Ezra's unfair assumptions about them had endangered everyone.

"So, what do we do now?" Ben asked, jumping when there came another bang at the wall.

Ezra stared at the door, silent. "...I don't know. Magic doesn't work on them.

Kiera felt his hopelessness drift into her as well.

Ben was the only one who stood firm. He shrugged, turned to a nearby table in this empty hallway they inhabited, and grabbed one of its legs. Then, with a loud crunch, he yanked it off and handed it to Kiera.

"So what if we can't use magic on them?" Ben asked, doing the same to the second table leg and handing it to Ezra. "We can still use it on ourselves, and nothing beats a good old bat to the face, right?" He held up his own third table leg and studied it. "Close enough."

"I can't use my magic," Ezra admitted quietly, and Kiera said the same.

"The fairies took it for themselves," she said glumly, feeling too weak to even carry the weapon.

"Well." Ben grinned, overcompensating to make up for their lack of energy. "I have enough magic to go around. Now, which do you prefer? Strength or elemental? I can only do so many spells at once, so..." He waited for them to answer, knowing they didn't have a choice. When neither of them said anything, he leaned forward. "We just have to hold the things off until backup arrives. That's it. How far away is your family, Ezra?"

"A twenty-minute drive, supposedly."

"Then we only have to survive for twenty minutes." As Ben finished his pep talk, Tucker joined them and said he told the security guards who would get to a speaker and warn everyone. True to his word, an alarm went off a second later. A booming voice warned everyone to stay in their rooms, not open any doors or windows, and arm themselves with something.

"What's the plan?" Tucker asked as Ben handed him the fourth table leg. He looked down at it in confusion, then a light bulb seemed to go off, and he nodded. "Doing things the old-fashioned way, are we?"

Kiera glanced at Ezra, who seemed resigned to it and was looking a little less glum.

"I'm guessing elemental will just strengthen them more," she said to Ben, answering his earlier question. "So strength might be the best option." That might even give more magic to the fairies on contact, but it was better than nothing. The fairies could steal away the magic either way. "Whenever you're ready."

24

Kiera prayed the sight when they opened that door a crack would be peaceful. They'd see nothing but an empty path, with clear air above it and silence abounding. That would give them an excuse to shut the door again and sit there for the next twenty minutes while they waited for the headmaster to arrive with something that would save them all.

Instead, the sight was dreadful.

The air was filled with those disgusting fairies, flying about and opening their mouths unnaturally wide to suck in the fresh air like they were drinking an ocean. A few of them had teenagers in their grip, their jaws strapped to the human's arms or legs like piranhas.

The air was also filled with the screams of young

men and women from the dorms. A few of them even ran into sight, dashing away from the fairies. Meanwhile, others tried to use magic to defend themselves—shooting balls of fire or lightning at the things. Of course, the elemental attacks did nothing to the fairies. Instead, the creatures absorbed the bright orbs shot at them, and it made their bodies increase in size. Then, the student who had used the magic would slump over, their magic and, therefore, their energy drained. This gave the fairies the perfect victim to leap on and start devouring.

It was utter chaos, and it made hot acid rise up Kiera's throat.

Tucker, ever the woman-saving hero, immediately grabbed a stone and hurled it at one of the fairies carrying a girl through the air. The rock connected with the fairy's head, probably led by a spell of Tucker's own making. It didn't make the fairy release its prey, but it did detach its mouth from the girl's shoulder to look at him.

Tucker looked down at his body, then turned to the others. "Using a projectile spell didn't weaken me. Use that to throw things at them." Then he shut the door once all four of them were out so the fairies couldn't enter the building.

Kiera nodded even though she had little to no magic left. Ezra did the same.

Luckily, Ben did have enough, just like he said, and as he charged toward a fairy hovering close to the ground with his weapon raised, he sent several nearby rocks toward the fairy in a pile. The stones hit its face just before he brought the chair leg down on its head. He was screaming a battle cry at the top of his lungs as he battered it.

The fairy didn't die when Ben hit it, but it did start to fly away, back toward the library. It was too fast for Ben to chase, especially with the added weight his magical muscles brought.

"Stay inside. Do not use magic except to create a barrier, a shield, or a self-enhancing protective spell," the voice over the intercoms said, confirming what they already knew. "Arm yourselves with physical objects."

As Kiera stood there, unsure what to do since she had no magic left and wasn't particularly strong, she saw the security guards finally run out into the fray, armed with actual swords and wearing uniforms that resembled both bulletproof vests and medieval armor. Their weapons had more of an impact when it came to hurting the fairies than a simple piece of wood or stone.

"You can go back inside if you need to," Ezra assured her before stepping forward to join Ben.

Kiera was tempted to. She'd never felt so helpless, even last semester when her skills were at their lowest. Now she had the ability to use spells but had no magic to do it with.

But as she watched the humans fight against the fairies and saw the monsters become bigger, stronger, and faster anytime they bit or even touched a human, she grit her teeth. She caused this chaos and would feel like a complete jerk if she just hid inside while everyone around her fought. No, she would do her best, even if it meant she lost magic forever.

"I'm with you," she told Ezra confidently and ran forward, the little bit of added muscle Ben gave her bringing her back to normal levels of energy.

Ezra just grinned and followed. Together, they started fighting off the fairies, heading toward the dorms and the library next to it.

They only needed fifteen more minutes before backup arrived.

25

Once again, time seemed to come to a standstill. Five minutes felt like five hours as Kiera and Ezra tried to beat down every fairy within reach. Thanks to their lack of magic within them, the fairies didn't seem to hunt them down the way they did Ben, Tucker, and the other security guards either. There was no benefit to it.

So, it was fairly easy to run up to a fairy, attack its arms and legs, and eventually stab its gaping mouth. The fairies would adapt quickly and fly out of reach, but just hitting them where it hurt was enough to stop them from hurting someone else for a little while.

By the time those five minutes were up, Kiera's arms were shaking from adrenaline, the fake muscles on her arms had worn off, and the top of her now bent table leg was black from whatever dark substance the fairies had beneath their stretched skin.

Ezra looked excited beside her. The rush from fighting and actually making an impact had him breathing heavily but also chuckling when they paused to catch their breath.

"This is almost fun," he confided in her, running a hand across his sweaty forehead and leaving a streak of black blood across it. "We should do this more often—"

Kiera was about to laugh when they heard an explosion, then the sound of splintering wood. It was coming from the library. She turned just in time to see the walls of the library burst outwards, showering the surrounding area with broken wood and shattered glass. A second after that, the roof rose and toppled to the side, allowing an enormous creature to rise up from within it.

It was the fairy that had first spoken to Kiera, though it was ten times larger, and its body had gone from thin and feminine to thick and animalistic. Its teeth had grown to the size of swords, and its eyes were now so big on its head that they covered not only the eye sockets but also the forehead. Its hair was barely clinging to its head now, and its limbs were covered in thick, scale-like flesh that had turned a glowing white.

"It almost makes me jealous," Ezra said with an exhausted sigh, clearly tired of dealing with all these escalations. "When we have magic, we're confined to using words to activate it. With these things, they can just use it to make themselves into giant monsters. How is that fair?"

Kiera had to agree. What made it worse was that giant thing had fed off of her magic specifically, so she was the reason it had gotten so big and powerful. She scoffed, disgusted by the sight of it, but she was too busy studying the creature and library to say anything aloud.

While most of the library had been destroyed, the far wall where the fairy door stood was still intact. She wasn't sure what she could do with that knowledge, but it felt important regardless.

As soon as the giant fairy revealed itself, the wounded ones flew back to it and, to Kiera's disgust, flew right into its skin like it was some fleshy vehicle for them to drive. The disgusting sound of wet and tearing skin made her want to vomit.

Now that most of the fairies around them were gone and the only ones still attacking were in the dorms, the rest of them congregated with the exception of Tucker, who headed off to find Sally and Meiying.

"Ben," Kiera said as soon as he ran up to them. There were a few security guards still around, armed with blackened swords, but they headed toward the dorms to help. Now it was just Ezra, Kiera, and a red-faced Ben. "Is there anything else you can tell us about the realm they trapped the fairies in? How they activated it, or what precautions they put in place?"

Ben furrowed his brow, thinking, then shrugged. "Just that everything in it had to be dead," he said.

Kiera looked down. So her being inside it, the only living thing truly could have been the catalyst that activated everything. Great. Now she had to find a way to fix that. They could wait for the Gillis family to arrive, but in ten minutes, that giant fairy could punch a hole in the dorms. It might even get bigger by then.

"Our little sticks won't do much against it," Ezra said and studied Ben's arm, which had a long, jagged cut in it. "And I'm guessing you've lost some of your magic too, so we can't do anything drastic."

"Right." Ben nodded, wincing as he looked down at his arm, eyes wide as though this was the first time he realized he had just a deep and jagged wound. "I hate to admit it, but I'm pretty spent."

As they spoke, Kiera focused on the library again. Once more, she was feeling that tug toward the door. However, this time, there was no sense of dread and wrongness about it. Instead, it felt like the door was requesting she fix it and use it for its intended purpose this time. There were no fairies prying at her mind and tempting her. This was just a genuine plea to fix things. The last bit of magic inside her nearly pushed her forward, using the last of its strength to give her purpose.

She knew what she had to do, though it would be risky.

Then again, anything was better than cowering here.

"I'm going into the library to fix the door and room," she told Ben and Ezra, cutting them off mid-conversation.

"What?" Ezra went pale, and he stepped toward her. "No you're not. That's suicide."

"Why would you do that?" Ben added.

"I have a feeling we'll still need that room intact and ready if we want the headmaster to lock the fairies up again," she said. "And my... I have a feeling I need to make everything inside it dead again." She didn't want to say her magic was telling her to do it. That would sound silly.

Ezra and Ben glanced at each other, considering it, but neither looked convinced.

"That giant fairy could step on you," Ben countered, pointing at it. It had taken a few steps away from the library, toward the dorms where all the fairies were swarming around like mosquitoes.

"But this is the only time that realm is empty," Kiera said. "Besides, I have you two to distract it, right?" She offered them a cheeky grin, knowing that offer to be heroes would bring Ben on board but Ezra? Not so much.

"We don't even know if that will work," Ezra countered. "Let's just wait for—"

"Did they even tell you what type of spell they plan to use?" she asked, frustrated by how little adults told them. She was sure their constant need to look down on Ezra was to blame for that part.

Ezra blinked rapidly. "They said they'd use the room," he admitted slowly, then groaned and gave in. "Fine. I'll protect you and hold them off the best I can. They're distracted anyway. Ben?" He turned toward Ben, for once not giving absolute orders right off the bat.

Ben's eyebrows rose, shocked by Ezra letting him do what he wanted. Then he looked down at the still intact table leg in his hand. "I think my magic's back for the most part." He paused, and his muscles got bigger again. "I'll distract them. How long do we have? Fifteen minutes?"

"Ten," Kiera said. "Maybe even less."

"That's plenty of time." Ben took one step away, ready to fight again, when he stopped. "Do you two have your magic back, though?"

Ezra shook his head, then looked at Kiera, who nodded slowly.

"I have enough," she said, knowing it to be true. She could feel the last bit of it still inside her, eager to be of use. Even if it wasn't enough, she would still use it as long as she could before it was gone for good.

"Alright." Ezra gave Ben a thumbs up, then turned to enter what was left of the library. "See you in ten minutes, Ben."

"Likewise." Ben saluted, then charged the dorm buildings, screaming as he went. He was almost comical in his actions. Kiera knew he was having the time of his life, getting to finally live out the actions of his comic book heroes.

Then, she and Ezra headed toward the door once more. Hopefully, this would be the last time they had to see it.

26

"I think this is the right thing to do," Kiera assured Ezra as they ran, dodging debris and staying out of sight of the gigantic fairy and its underlings. "The door itself wasn't made by the fairies. It was designed to keep them contained inside. That means the thing that lured me in wasn't the door, as I originally thought, but the fairies inside it."

"Well, the door did a crummy job of keeping them secure," Ezra muttered grumpily as they ran. His emotions were at their limit. First, he had the stress of his family, then his (not) girlfriend was in danger, and now they were all fighting man-eating fairies. "Though I suppose the magic may have worn down over time, or the renovation accidentally weakened its foundations or something. I'm still pissed at whoever decided to magically change the building and didn't check to ensure he or she didn't disrupt anything."

Kiera couldn't help chuckling at his little complaints. They felt so strange amidst all the shouts, swishes of swords, and stomping of fairy feet. The reluctant smile Ezra gave back to her made her forget their surroundings for a moment, and it was just the two of them on an adventure together, saving the world.

Then they reached the door, and Kiera had to focus again. It was still there, green as ever. The plants weren't moving anymore, though.

Ezra moved the door open with his foot, and they looked inside. What was once brown and barren was once again blooming and lively again. The grass had even more flower beds than before. There were even leaves sprouting from the trunks of the trees rather than just the branches above.

"If my uncle plans to put them back in here," Ezra commented, on board with Kiera's idea finally, "We'll need to make this place devoid of life. I think you were right after all."

More like her magic was right, which gave her the intuition.

"Okay. I'll guard the front while you drain the life. Let's do it for real this time," he said, making a small joke of their previous failure. "Let's hope that without the fairies around, it'll actually work."

"Agreed." Then they did just that, going their separate ways.

The little world became blissful as she started draining the life, starting with the grass under her feet and slowly working her way out. It took a very long time, as the tiny tendrils of magic were few and weak. They started with just a few blades per second and had to very slowly snake their way around. Luckily, Kiera couldn't feel herself draining this time as she used the magic. The world she was in didn't seem to protest either. The area around her seemed to breathe easier as the green slowly faded away. Perhaps brown and dead was its natural state, and it preferred it that way.

"I'm sorry for ruining your... you," she whispered to the realm as the edges of the grass wilted. "We can hopefully let you continue your job once all this is done." It must have taken a lot of magic to make this place. It's a shame a simple touch was enough to make it lose its purpose.

She was working her way up the trees, over halfway done with her work, when she heard a grunt outside, followed by a shriek and the dull thump of wood meeting flesh.

One of the fairies was back, and Ezra was fighting it.

❦

FOR A SECOND, KIERA STOOD THERE ON THE dead, crunchy grass, debating whether to continue or go out and help Ezra. In the end, her care for him decided for her, and she didn't do anything to end the spell but did head out with her bent piece of wood, ready to swing it at anything that shrieked.

As she pushed the door open, she heard another crunch and stepped forward just in time to see Ezra bring his weapon down on a smaller fairy's head. That sickening sound of bone breaking came from its head, but the indent Ezra had created in what should be its skull didn't stop it from laughing maniacally and grabbing both of his hands with its own. As soon as it did so, digging its jagged nails into his skin and drawing blood, Ezra slumped forward. It was draining what was left of him.

"Get your hands off him!" Kiera shouted to pump herself up, then she smacked it across the face with her stick and kicked it with her boot in the stomach since making contact with her boot wouldn't drain her.

The creature released Ezra's arms, making him crumble to the ground, then it turned to her and continued laughing, black spittle hitting the ground between them.

Kiera stepped back, preparing to swing at it again, when the open door suddenly closed slightly, hitting the fairy in the side and knocking it several feet over where it hit the ground.

Kiera's eyes widened, surprised that the door was helping her. Then she had the brilliant idea of grabbing a nearby bookshelf on the wall and tipping it forward, so it landed on the fairy. Since the bookshelf was already damaged and part of it had fallen off, it wasn't as heavy and therefore was easier to push. The tall structure landed with a satisfying thud, crushing the fairy's legs and keeping it trapped down there. It screamed and scratched at the wood and metal but couldn't move out from under it.

"Just stay down," Kiera grumbled. She then grabbed Ezra and tried pulling him into the fairy realm, or rather a prison. As she did so, he blinked and gasped, sucking in air like he'd been without oxygen the entire time. Then he looked around for the fairy.

"I've trapped it," Kiera said, handing him her

stick. "And I'm almost done in here. Can you stand?"

He nodded and looked at his watch. "Five minutes," he told her. "I wish I could help."

Kiera immediately started reciting the spell of death again, hoping the look of appreciation she gave him told him that his presence here was enough to make her feel safe. Then she focused all her magic on the trees again as he walked out of the door a second time.

The small space felt even more welcoming now. It was strange that think that such a dead, lifeless place without even a breeze somehow felt homey. It must be the strange life that the space itself bore, given a purpose that it knew it could fulfill again once it was back to its natural, lifeless state.

"Almost there," she whispered between spell verses. She'd said the spell so many times now that it felt like a song, albeit a choppy one without rhymes or rhythm. Without the noise of battle outside, everything felt peaceful.

Three more trees to go.

She heard a bang outside and turned slightly but kept chanting.

Two more trees.

Ezra started to say something, then grunted.

There was a loud thump of him falling to the ground, then silence.

One more tree.

Her magic wound around the tree like a slinky, traveling up until it reached the branches. Then, it had to travel down each branch individually, eating at the leaves until they were brown before continuing its ascension.

Five more branches.

Four more.

She kept glancing over her shoulder at the door, trying to peer through the crack. It had shut itself again as she entered. Maybe it was protecting her from the outside. Who knows?

Three more.

Two.

The door was yanked open from the outside and wobbled, nearly getting ripped off its hinges.

One more branch.

Her body froze as a huge eyeball peered through the doorway, all black and writhing. Even though it was all one color, she could see it moving, studying the room before landing on her. Then the eyeball went up and out of sight. The head it was attached to had moved away.

Kiera held her breath as the magic finished its journey along the final branch. Then, it zipped back toward her. She couldn't see the magic but could always feel its presence, and as it came back to her, she felt its comfort inside her like a warm campfire in the middle of winter.

Then, a large white hand reached through the doorway and grabbed her, tugging her out through the door and into the air.

The giant fairy had her in its grasp. It was even bigger now, and its grip was so tight that no struggling could even move her fingers. Kiera recoiled as she looked at the skin on its bare stomach, and she saw things writhing around beneath it. Their forms were of other, smaller fairies. For some reason, they had all congregated inside this one giant one. Perhaps they were here to drop off the magic they'd procured, like bees dropping off pollen in the hive. That would explain why this thing became so powerful at such a fast rate.

The stench of death from its mouth was even worse now. Who knew magic could have such a vile smell? Though the fact that I was mixed with blood might be the real cause of that.

As it rose to its full height and carried Kiera off with her, she could see several things below her. The first was Ezra, once again unconscious in front of the golden door. The next was the security guards and Ben, who were in a similar state.

The only people still awake and fighting were Tucker, his friends Sally and Meiying, and a few other students and professors. All of them were bleeding from somewhere, and more than one had those jagged cuts and scratches on their faces that would likely never heal fully. They were fighting against a few fairies, who would fly above them and occasionally dart forward to snag a bite before retreating into the air again. By the looks of it, though, the humans were weakening and would collapse soon.

Kiera glanced back up at the fairy. From her height, she was taller than the highest staff building. Just a few minutes ago, this thing hadn't been as tall as the library. How big would it get if it sucked up all the magic in the whole school? How many magic-wielders would it take to bring it down then?

She had no idea what to do against it other than to cry out as it squeezed her. She could feel its cold skin against hers, sapping out the last bit of magic that had held out for so long. Then, she expected it to drop her so she'd splatter on the ground, or it would squash her between its fingers. Her last bit of magic was the only thing keeping her from those two futures.

"What do I do?" she shouted, directing her

words at the professors, the door, the magic inside her, anybody.

There was no answer.

She had no solution now. There was no special idea that sprang into her head that would fix this. She had no sudden bout of energy that allowed her to best the beast.

She'd done stupid things twice in a row, and it had led to this situation. She had put the boy she loved and her best friend in danger. She deserved whatever she got.

But she still didn't want to die.

27

The fairy didn't even say anything to her as it breathed down on her. There was no more reason to manipulate her or convince her to come. The fairies were free and could do as they pleased now.

However, Kiera did see its tight skin wrinkle slightly as it squeezed her. It was taking a long time to get at her magic too. What was taking so long?

The monster seemed to be thinking the same thing as it started shaking her, its mouth open in visible frustration.

"Come out," it finally said, its voice hissing and all snake now. There was no more beautiful siren song. "Come out!" it shouted eventually, getting hot and searing spit all over Kiera's face and hair.

Kiera's magic resisted, as though acting on its own. Then, it finally left her, entering the fairy.

This was it. She was dead.

Kiera closed her eyes, scrunching down to anticipate the final squeeze or incoming drop.

Then, her magic zipped back into her, and it brought all of her original magic with her.

As her energy returned, she opened her eyes in surprise and looked up at the fairy , which wasn't looking at her now but at something on the ground. Kiera did the same and had to squint at the three figures walking toward her. Two were tall and clearly male, while the third was shorter and had a feminine walk. Who was that? They had to be responsible for giving back her magic.

The fairy growled, completely bear-like in its sound, and then the dreaded action happened. It dropped her.

Kiera screamed, feeling the wind rush through her hair. She tried to recall the spell for "Feather Fall," a spell that would make her float down so she wouldn't get hurt. Even as she said the first words, though, she knew the drop was too fast to give her time to say it all. That was the drawback of magic. Unless someone was a master, they were limited by how fast they could speak.

One of the men on the ground wasn't, though.

She heard him shout words in an ancient language. Then she felt something soft beneath her. A second later, her body came to rest on the ground.

She sat up, recognizing the voice and feeling immediate anxiety in her chest from it. It was Kent, Ezra's brother. He'd finally arrived and saved her life on top of it.

The giant fairy stomped toward the three figures, one of whom Kiera now knew was Kent, but the being seemed to be shrinking as it approached. The ancient words the other two people were saying was slowing it down and bringing it back to its original size.

"Ezra?" Kiera's thoughts immediately turned to him. She scrambled to her feet and headed for the door where she last saw him. Sure enough, there he was, but he was awake yet again and was crawling toward the action instead. He only stopped when he saw her, and relief washed over his face.

"I thought you were dead," he said, rising. "I saw you fall."

"Your brother saved me," she said, still in shock that it had happened. "And I'm guessing your uncle's with him too."

Ezra looked past her and nodded, then squinted. "Who's that third person?"

"I don't know." Kiera found herself unconsciously reaching for his hand, and she didn't breathe again until she had it. Both of their palms were cakey with blood now, and she could feel a cut through two of his fingers. She started healing him at once as they cautiously walked closer to the three people and the giant they were bringing down together.

When they were close enough to make out the face of the third person, Kiera stopped walking in astonishment. It was a young woman, Kiera's age, with dark skin and pretty curled hair that was longer than the last time they met. This was the girl who cursed boys into stone using dark, twisted magic. It was the serial killer from last semester, Erin, and she was working with Kent and the headmaster.

"What's she doing here?" Kiera whispered in disbelief. After looking on for a few more seconds, she realized the girl was wearing handcuffs, though that wouldn't stop her from reciting spells, which she was doing right now.

"Maybe they need her dark magic expertise," Ezra muttered, though he didn't sound happy about it. "Maybe she was all they had in close proximity."

"Can we help?" Kiera asked, and Ezra shook his head.

"Not unless we figure out what they're doing," he said. "And it looks like they've got it handled."

And he was right. The fairy kept shrinking and eventually split up into multiple fairies again, though even those ones shrank down from human size to half that until they were no bigger than one's palm.

Only then did Kent pull a tiny, black box from his pocket and whisper something into it. As soon as he did, it grew and enveloped all the little fairies before sealing itself off.

"Where's the door?" Kent shouted to anyone nearby. He spun around, angrily scanning his surroundings for people not on the floor, and he scowled when he spotted Kiera and Ezra. "The door?" he repeated, his voice now dripping with venom.

Kiera stepped back and pointed to it, immensely glad she had cleared it of life earlier. That would lower the risk of the fairies escaping whatever that box was.

The headmaster stayed with Erin as Kent ran toward Kiera and Ezra, then past them into the grove. He peeked inside first, probably making sure everything was good and dead, then tossed the box in. Kiera noticed that he didn't set foot inside when he threw the box, and he also didn't touch the door when he closed it. He used a spell instead.

Then he and the headmaster started casting a protective spell around the door, creating a shimmering white field that surrounded it so no person or thing could get inside. Only after that was done did they stop to take a breath.

"Is it over?" Erin asked, sounding bored despite taking down a fairy the size of a small tower. She barely glanced at Kiera and Ezra as she walked past them to reach Kent, though Kiera got the feeling she was intentionally avoiding their eyes.

"Yes," Kent said, turning fiery eyes on her. He then muttered a single word, and her mouth sealed shut, followed by being covered with a metal contraption that sprang from the back of her neck. "Uncle, I assume you can escort her out of here now? I'll keep an eye on the door to make sure no more imbeciles—" He gave Kiera and Ezra a pointed look. "—get their grubby hands on it again."

Kiera felt her throat dry up, knowing he was completely in the right this time.

Both Kent and the headmaster looked exhausted, like they'd been up all night. Maybe they had, looking for solutions while Kiera and Ezra assumed they were lounging about doing nothing.

Kent had dark circles under his eyes, and they were bloodshot, too, making the anger pop out even more on his face.

"What's she doing here?" Ezra asked his uncle as the headmaster led Erin away. "I thought she was in juvenile detention for witches." Or prison.

The headmaster paused, glanced at Ezra, and shook his head, looking annoyed by the interruption. "She was the closest person we had who knew how to make spells that could avoid using regular magic. We needed something the fairies couldn't drain, and she had it." He then held up a small sack he'd been hiding in his coat pocket. It was full of dead animals. Mice, birds, snakes, and pigs. "She sent the magic through these so the fairies could only drain them instead of us. The spells she used also had..." He paused as though debating whether he should tell his students about this. "Well, she's very good at what she does. If she becomes an upstanding citizen again, she'll prove to be a valuable ally."

"And even if she doesn't follow the rules, we'll still use her," Kent added from afar, making the hairs on Kiera's neck stand up. He was detestable. No wonder Ezra didn't like him.

Satisfied with his own explanation, the headmaster nodded goodbye to Ezra and headed off with Erin in front of them. Erin didn't say goodbye at all, which didn't surprise Kiera.

"Ezra," Kent said to Ezra, and Kiera prepared to leave. "Once all of this is over and done with, and I finish cleaning up your mess, you and I are going to have a very long talk." He glared at his brother, then at Kiera too, before turning back to the door. The conversation was over before it had even begun.

Kiera glanced at Ezra and could already see the color leaving his body. His brother seemed to stress him out more than killer fairies did.

"Let's go make sure Tucker and Ben are okay," she told him quietly, still holding his hand and pulling him away from Kent. "And Sally and Meiying too."

Ezra nodded, and they did so, glad to find everyone alive and well, albeit pretty beat up. It proved a good chance for Kiera to practice her medicine spells on them. However, the knowledge that all of this was Kiera's fault never left her mind, and she could tell from his eyes that Kent felt the same.

She wondered if she'd be punished for this. Probably not, since the fairies were technically at fault, but she could still be expelled. However, she was sure the professors knew her first encounter with the door wasn't her fault. Whoever renovated the building would probably take the brunt of the punishment.

The real worry was what would happen to Ezra. His family was sure to hear about this and the trouble he'd caused. They didn't seem the type to let people off lightly, especially the son they had placed so many expectations on.

28

The school closed down for the next three days since there were around thirty students with serious injuries and twenty others with cuts and bruises that needed healing. Thanks to the healing magic-wielders that were brought in for the situation, no one ended up with any permanent damage, but Kiera was told the new scars on her arms, legs, and face would take years to totally fade. The scars looked more like small holes across her skin, like a corn field from above. It wasn't pretty, but luckily most of that was on parts of her arms and legs that would be hidden by pants and sleeves anyway.

On the third day of school, once she was taken back from the magical hospital, instead of going to class like normal, Kiera instead woke to someone knocking on the door and found her favorite professor from last semester, Professor Smith, standing there in a suit.

"Hello, Kiera," he said, ignoring her rumpled pajamas and unkempt hair. "I'm here to have a little... discussion with you before you start your day." His previously balding head had full hair again, which either meant he got a normal surgery with implants or he'd used some type of hair growth spell. Either way, it looked both nice and strange to see him with hair again.

"Am I in trouble?" Kiera asked quietly. She knew Ezra was. She'd barely been able to talk to him in person, and the few texts he said implied he was spending most of his time receiving lectures from his uncle. She thought she'd managed to avoid all that. Apparently not.

"No, you're not in trouble," Professor Smith assured her. "But the school board has assigned me to discuss what happened to you and the door since you were the first to encounter it." He paused to think for a moment. "There is also the matter of... discipline as well, which we'll discuss. Instead of going to class today, I'd like you to come to my office in forty-five minutes. Do you still remember where it is?"

Kiera nodded, already feeling dread fill her gut.

"Good. See you then." He smiled, that constant look of understanding on his face lowering her guard even though her brain told her she was about to get in trouble or expelled for what she did.

She'd been to Professor Smith's office a few times. It was a small room with nothing particularly out of the ordinary until you opened any of the drawers. There was a desk with a few locked drawers that she assumed held magical items that did wondrous things. There were also a few cupboards above the desk, which she'd seen inside on her previous visits. Those contained a lot of magical components, like the aforementioned orc and goblin body parts, as well as preserved animal bodies in glass jars or dried boxes. As Kiera sat down, Professor Smith opened one of these cupboards and pulled a small box with a bone inside that definitely belonged to a fairy's wing. It was white with some patches of black that looked like mold.

After setting it down in front of her, he took a seat and gestured toward it.

"I took this from the scene of the crime," he said, "But that's all we managed to find that proves anything happened at all. Due to that, and most of the cameras being destroyed during the fight, I'd like you to tell me everything that happened from start to finish. We heard a lot from your friends, including the Gillis boy, but all accounts say you were the most connected to everything, so..." He paused to bring out a small, black recording device. "I hope you don't mind if I record everything?"

She gulped, knowing that if she told the truth, he'd have evidence of her admitting to what could potentially be a crime against the magical world. However, lying wouldn't do her any good, and he might even have a truth spell on her right now that would tell him when she lied.

So, she said it was fine, which made him look relieved.

The next twenty minutes were spent telling him every detail, from the dreams that started it all, to entering the room, to the façade of the fairies, and the eventual break-in that kicked off the fairy escape. She didn't spare any details, and Professor Smith would sometimes smile sadly when she described doing something she knew she shouldn't have. Only after her story was done did he speak.

"This specific type of fairy is known for its telepathy and ability to burrow into the mind," he told her calmly, assuredly. "They cannot control their victims, but they can encourage certain actions and elicit certain emotions. No one can blame someone as young as you for doing what you did under that kind of influence—especially when you didn't know what was causing it."

Kiera shifted uncomfortably in her seat. Even though she was eighteen now, she felt like both a child and an adult at this moment.

"But I'm still the one who did it," she protested quietly, crossing her arms. "So, what is the school going to do about this? And me?"

"Well, as I'm sure you saw and heard, they're renovating the building again since it practically needs to be rebuilt from scratch. They're able to relocate the door somewhat and are building some steel walls around it, so there's no risk of anyone getting in again. The door needs to have zero contact with life, which requires blocking out every person and animal that comes nearby."

Kiera had already heard that from the rumors spreading throughout the dorms. Ezra's brother Kent had been supervising the whole thing, and she didn't even mind now. He clearly knew what he was doing in that regard.

"As for you, the school wants me to warn you that if you ever encounter something strange, supernatural, paranormal, or just slightly dangerous, you need to inform an adult with authority instead of touching it yourself."

"Right." She felt a lump forming in her throat, dreading the next words.

"As long as you genuinely understand and follow those rules and swear to never put yourself or others in danger again, the school will not take any actions against you."

What? They weren't expelling her? She was at a loss for words.

"They won't even put anything on your record," he added when she didn't say anything. "Is that satisfactory?"

"Uh... Yes! Of course!" She was just too shocked to speak, was all. The headmaster had really let her get away with no more than a "Be more careful next time" warning? She was shocked.

Maybe Ezra had something to do with it. Perhaps he took the blame or convinced his family to go easy on her.

"I will say, off the record," he said as he turned off his recorder and leaned forward on his desk, smiling like a proud parent. "I am impressed that you and Ezra knew to clear the room of life so the fairies could be returned without issue. I heard the delay removing all the light could have caused would have given the fairies a chance to escape again, so you did a respectable job. Just try to prevent such emergencies before they happen, rather than after, next time."

"Right." She grinned back. "I'm glad I got at least one thing right."

"Keep using that creativity and practicing your spells," he told her. "You have a talent for magic. I can't wait to see it thrive."

29

That afternoon, she finally got to see Ezra in person again. He texted her asking to meet up in front of the library, or rather what was left and being rebuilt. She found him sitting on a bench in front of it, watching both the crane carrying rubble away and the magic-wielders using telekinesis to lift things into place. It was an interesting combination of magic and everyday tools at work.

"I'm surprised they brought a crane," she remarked as she sat next to him. He still didn't look that good. He was still pale and with dark circles. His smile when he saw her brightened up his face, though.

"They don't want to risk using magic only when that door is still nearby," he told her, gingerly wrapping his arm around her shoulder as she settled in. Then he refocused on where the door used to be and stared. "I wanted to keep an eye on it," he added quietly. "Just in case something went wrong."

"Well." Kiera tried to stay positive. "At least no one got hurt. It could have been much worse, right?"

He shrugged. "We were lucky the fairies had no reason to kill anybody. They just wanted our magic and nothing else. Cutting us up was just a means to get at the magic within." He shuddered. "If they were planning to kill us, though, none of us would have survived."

She hated to admit it, but he was right. So far, they'd only encountered non-lethal enemies. The first person, Erin, was called a "serial killer," but she gave them plenty of time to stop her. These fairies also caused some damage, but it wasn't anything that couldn't be fixed.

If Kiera ever encountered an actual threat, she doubted she'd be able to stop it. That's why she had to take Professor Smith's warning very seriously.

She looked over at Ezra and tried to picture a life without him, or worse, a life where she accidentally caused his death. It hurt to imagine.

"That's not to say I'm not glad we're all alive," Ezra added quietly, glancing at her. Their eyes met for a moment, and she knew he'd been thinking about the exact same thing she was—imagining a world without her and being glad it didn't exist.

He leaned forward slightly, opening his mouth to say something, but before he could speak or move any closer, Kiera heard Kent's voice calling from afar, and they both pulled apart before the brother could get there.

Unlike his little brother, Kent looked happier than ever. He was wearing a mahogany brown suit, which made him look very much like an inspector. It was probably the appearance he was going for since Tucker mentioned he was often here, supervising the construction and sometimes doing it himself.

"I thought that was you," Kent said. His cold voice from the fairy attack was once again replaced by his fake, friendly professor tone. The smile never met his eyes, though. While he looked to be in a good mood, it clearly wasn't because of Ezra's or her presence. "I'm glad you're here, Ezra. You and I need to have a talk."

A strong sense of déjà vu from earlier today struck her. However, the look of pure hatred Kent directed toward her didn't match. She bristled.

"What else is there to say?" Ezra asked quietly.

"Uncle Phil already gave me several lectures. What more could you possibly have to say?"

"He lectured you about your endangerment of the school and its students," Kent said in a condescending tone. "I am here to lecture you about more... personal matters." Another pointed look toward Kiera. "Alone."

Ezra looked at Kiera, unwilling to leave, but when Kent's face scrunched up in annoyance, Ezra finally relented. They walked to the other end of the library remains.

Kiera stayed seated and planned to do nothing, but when she saw the two brothers start to get heated—with both of them raising their voices and arms in the air—she couldn't resist listening in. She uttered a small spell that would enhance her hearing, even though it technically wasn't allowed on campus for privacy reasons, and listened.

Kent was doing most of the talking. "Have you not seen articles published about our school? Not only were the magic academia papers talking about it, but even normal, mainstream media made articles. Do you know how that looks? Can you imagine how our uncle feels to have his name plastered everywhere alongside *killer fairies* and *student scars*? You and your girlfriend's names don't appear at all, yet you're the ones to blame."

She heard nothing from Ezra for a moment. He must be taking a second to collect his thoughts. "I hope the articles mentioned how Uncle Phil authorized someone renovating the library without checking the original blueprints or even bothering to walk around to make sure nothing was amiss," Ezra fired back. "Whoever did it clearly didn't even walk through the library once since a giant glowing door was overlooked."

"Oh. You're so right. Well, do you know what a smart person does when you find a giant, glowing, magical door? They tell a professor. They don't walk in like an idiot and endanger everyone around them."

"Are you seriously blaming students for something the board caused?"

"No. I'm saying your girlfriend was acting like a moron, and you can be sure I'll be relaying everything that happened to our parents. Every single minute detail, Ezra. They need to know what kind of person you allow yourself to associate with."

"Are you seriously going to whine to mom and dad about Kiera?" Ezra scoffed. "How old are you again?"

"It's all fun and games until you or your friends get someone killed. You wouldn't be laughing if those fairies were actually lethal now, would you?

Your caretakers deserve to know what kind of influences you keep around. Their future heir should have more caution, especially when it comes to magic. We aren't normal humans, Ezra. You seem to so often forget that."

"I have never forgotten that. I take magic seriously—"

"Is that why your grades are dropping?"

"...I have a 3.9 GPA. I hardly call that dropping."

"But it's a sign of things to come. If your girlfriend's 2.9 is any indication—"

"Kiera and I are separate people, Kent."

"I don't think it's a coincidence that you stopped studying after you met her."

"I didn't stop studying!"

"Then explain why your grades dropped."

There was another pregnant pause, then Ezra spoke again. His voice was level now, hiding his anger. "You know what I think, Kent? I don't think you care about the students at all or what happened to them. You don't care about me, Kiera, or any of my other friends. All you care about is making me look bad to our parents so it'll make you look good."

"Why should I care what they think of me?" Kent scoffed, but Ezra didn't let up.

"If you actually cared about me and my studies, you'd help me instead of—"

"There's no point helping you if you surround yourself with people who will bring you down."

Kiera's heart ached. Initially, the pain came because the brother so outwardly hated her, and if that was the case, the chances of forming a long-term relationship with Ezra felt completely out of reach.

However, she hurt for Ezra much more. She loved her parents, and if any of them spoke to her the way Kent spoke to Ezra, she'd never want to go home or be around them. She might even lose the will to try working hard at all. Ezra was strong to keep persevering despite dealing with people like this. It was a wonder Ezra's hair hadn't started falling out.

"Choose better friends to hang out with," Kent said, beginning to walk away. "It's for your own good."

"And I'm warning you to back off," Ezra replied quietly, shoulders slumped in defeat. "Goodbye, brother."

Kiera stiffened as Kent walked past, but he didn't even acknowledge her as he left. That was probably for the best.

Once Kent was gone, she went to Ezra at the

same time he was returning to her, so they met in the middle. Before he could say anything, she swept him into a hug and just squeezed, not bothering to say, "Your brother's an idiot" or "You weren't in the wrong." She was sure it wouldn't help.

All he needed to know was, "I'm here for you."

"Thanks." He hugged her back, but when she looked at him, he was staring past her, already thinking things through.

"Now that everything's cleared up," she continued quietly. "Maybe we can start those study sessions again?"

"Sure, though maybe not as frequent this time." AKA, he needed to study on his own to catch up to his family's mounting expectations. What made it worse was he'd be doing it for her to prove she wasn't bringing him down.

She so desperately wanted to tell him she loved him and assure him that nothing mattered as long as they were together. So many sappy lines from romance movies were going through her head, but none of them would actually solve this problem. This was between him and his family, and at the end of the day, what his parents thought about her really didn't matter. If they judged Ezra solely on someone else, that was their own problem. She couldn't change that.

"Are you okay?" she asked finally.

"Yeah." He gave a forced laugh. "It's just my brother being controlling as always. Don't let his dull attitude bother you. He's like that to everyone. Rude, that is."

She knew it was more than that but appreciated that Ezra was trying to keep her out of it. "Okay. Good." She sighed, pressing her face into his shoulder. "I'm still worried about you, though."

"Don't be. I can manage everything." His confidence was so strong that she almost believed him. "Let's just focus on getting through to final exams, okay?"

"Right."

She now knew there would be no discussion of relationships or dating or getting closer for now. It stung a little to know that their relationship had been halted before it even began, thanks to a nagging brother and some fairies.

She didn't mind waiting, though. Ezra was worth it.

30

The rest of that semester was largely uneventful, at least when compared to skin-ripping fairies. However, it wasn't without stress. While Kiera had figured out what worked best for her in terms of studying and she continued to get along with her friends well, she still had to spend a large amount of her time poring over books.

Though Sally and Meiying would sometimes invite her for a girl's night out and Ben would try to convince her to attend a superhero movie with him, she would often have to reject them. Her grades were at risk of dropping. She had promised herself that she'd at least get a 3.0 GPA or higher in order to prove to Ezra's family that she was worthy of being his girlfriend.

That required a lot of work, thanks to her struggles with reading and retaining information that couldn't be practiced regularly. And the more complex spells became, the less she could practice them without risk of endangering something around her.

So, she did end up going out sometimes and enjoying the university life she had heard so much about—attending small parties with her friends and going out to the nearby human town Sunswept Ridge to do normal, human things like eating in restaurants, attending films or plays, and visiting the beach. However, she still spent a huge amount of time in the newly renovated library or her dorm, repeating senseless words for hours on end. The only consolation was that she'd only have to do a few more years of this.

The other reason the semester flew by so quickly and uneventfully was that she didn't get to see Ezra much outside of classes. He was equally busy with studying, if not more so, and his brother would often drag him away to get in some extra tutoring sessions that would leave Ezra pale, droopy-eyed, and jumpy.

The time they did get to spend together, though, was lovely, and Kiera could tell it would ease his mind from all the worries his brother caused. They went on exactly five dates during the semester, though neither of them officially called it a date, and it never led to anything more. One time they went fishing together in a pond on the school grounds. Another time was going to the movies to see a historical drama. The third date was spent in Ben's room, babysitting his niece while he went to see a movie he claimed would only be available on that day. The fourth was spent at the beach with Tucker, Sally, and Meiying, but Kiera and Ezra spent most of it alone.

Then, the final date was a small dinner in Sunswept Ridge the day before graduation. Those who had passed with high enough grades were allowed to continue into Dreadmore Academy's second year, in which students focused even more heavily on their major and prepared for further education. If a student so chose, their third year and beyond could be spent at Dreadmore, specializing in necromancy or specific classes in wizardry. If they wanted to specialize in a form of magic Dreadmore didn't offer, they could be transferred to another university, but the grades and prestige from Dreadmore would offer them huge scholarships and advantages later on.

That meant even if Kiera chose to transfer to a different university that offered healing magic specialization, Dreadmore would still prove to be a huge asset down the line. Employers didn't care what you did at Dreadmore, so long as you attended. The name itself was what mattered, which was why Ezra's uncle was so concerned about protecting its legacy.

That dinner was spent discussing just that: their futures. While Kiera was beginning to lean toward medicine and healing, Ezra seemed more and more unsure about his future in necromancy. Kiera suspected that was Kent's fault, but she didn't say anything because she knew bringing up that man's name would make Ezra shut down again. She didn't want that, especially since they'd be going their separate ways after graduation.

"We'd better stop talking about magic," Ezra whispered suddenly, smirking while giving a comical nod toward the people seated behind Kiera.

They were currently sitting in a small restaurant that served fish and chips, along with a plethora of drinks neither of them was legally old enough to drink yet. The air smelled of oil and fried potatoes, while the only other customers in the building were noticeably quiet. Kiera figured out why when she glanced over her shoulder.

The middle-aged couple behind them was leaning closer to her and Kiera, their ears almost turned sideways to eavesdrop. As soon as Kiera turned toward them, both the man and woman rushed to look as nonchalant as possible while shoving fried fish into their mouths.

Kiera looked back at Ezra, then giggled. "I forget how abnormal magic is outside of Dreadmore," she commented as she finished her final fries. "You'd think they would be, too, since the school's only a few miles away." They had taken a bus to get here, and it would be arriving again in thirty minutes, so they'd have to end this meal shortly anyway.

"My uncle says he tries to keep the school and this town separate," Ezra said, his smile already fading at the mention of family yet again. "He doesn't want them to start snooping or spread false rumors that would sully the school's reputation."

"Of course, of course." Kiera wasn't surprised and frankly didn't want to hear about it any more than he did. "So, we have thirty minutes. What do you want to do? Sit here or go stand out there and wait?"

Ezra grinned, more like a naughty child this time, and leaned back in his leather booth. "I learned a traveling spell. It'll make your hair look like it's been turned into a nest for birds, but it'll get us there without needing to crowd into a smelly bus."

"After Professor Stencil's teleportation demonstration backfired, I'm not sure I want to attempt any more high-level spells today," Kiera answered. The item her professor had attempted to teleport, a pencil, had ended up burnt to a crisp on both ends. Not even Professor Stencil could explain what went wrong.

"You don't trust me?" Ezra teased.

"I don't trust magic sometimes. It has a mind of its own," she replied honestly. "Besides, if we did that, our time together would be over much sooner."

He paused as though the thought hadn't crossed his mind. "We'll still visit each other over the summer, won't we?" His voice got quieter and became filled with a soft whine of loneliness. "I'll spend most of it studying, but..." His voice trailed off, and he stared at her a little too long. He was waiting for her to confirm that she wanted to spend more time together.

Kiera leaned back in her booth, too, mimicking his stance. His brother had probably put it into his head that they weren't fit to be together. She wouldn't be surprised if Kent convinced Ezra that Kiera didn't like him at all. That might explain all the dates but never using any labels of boyfriend and girlfriend.

"If you want to stop hanging out," he began quietly, likely assuming her silence was a rejection. "Then I understand."

"I don't want to stop," she said immediately, making him jolt slightly. His eyes lit up. "I don't care what your brother says about us. I enjoy spending time with you, and I plan to do it as much as I can during the summer." Her words came out so confident that it surprised her. A year ago, she never would have spoken this way.

The corner of his mouth jerked upward. "I'm glad," he said quietly. "Sometimes, I'm not sure. You're pretty hard to read."

Was she? She'd always assumed her crush on him was written all over her face. That's what Ben always said. But then again, Ben and Ezra had different intentions. Ben just wanted an excuse to tease her and would do so no matter how she felt, while Ezra was the one seriously trying to figure her out and vice versa.

At that moment, she considered just bringing up their relationship then and there. She wanted to know if he liked her or, rather, liked her enough to ignore his family's expectations.

But then her conscience pulled her back. She

couldn't ask him to decide between her and his family right now. Besides, they'd be miles apart for most of the summer. It was better to figure things out when they could meet regularly in person.

Sure, she might just be making up excuses to avoid the inevitable, but for now, everything made sense in her head.

"I'd like to hang out during the summer," she said finally. "As much as we possibly can."

"I'm glad." He fiddled with the ends of his sleeves, the teasing tone gone. "And maybe after the summer, we can... talk more about this." He gestured to the space between them. "After I deal with my family."

Her heart lit up. He'd just confirmed everything she was thinking about. That was a huge relief. "Yes. Let's do that."

Their moment was interrupted by a beeping from Ezra's watch, informing them the bus would be here soon.

"That was fast," Ezra muttered as they rushed to clear their plates and get out of there. His words applied to more than just the bus. Kiera felt like the last semester went by in a flash. She hoped summer would, too, because as much as she enjoyed the break, she couldn't wait to be back in that booth, spending another hour talking with Ezra about anything and everything. He was so easy to talk to and made her feel like she was the funniest, most entertaining person in the world.

As she followed him out of the restaurant, she stared at his broad back and the scar on his neck from the fairies. She almost lost him to those monsters, and she might really lose him again if she let Kent and his parents get in her way. She'd have to do everything in her power to protect him, both physically and mentally. She hoped by the time the next semester came around, she'd be brave enough to talk back to Kent and whoever else she needed to if it meant proving to Ezra that he was loved and should be allowed to follow whatever path he chose.

She'd already become ten times braver over the year. Facing off against the fairies had proven that. There had to be even more bravery inside her, just waiting for the right moment to come out.

31

Students of Dreadmore Academy could apparently go through anywhere from three to five different graduations, depending on the path they took. Today, Kiera would be going through her first: the prerequisite graduation, meaning she managed to pass their tests and was allowed to officially put "Dreadmore alumni" on her resume.

The graduation ceremony wasn't anything special. There were no dragons or magical fireworks or potions to drink that signified their ability to study. All that happened was the students were led to a large stage that had been placed in the school gardens. Then, in front of all the parents who attended, they would accept a *First Year Diploma* and return to their seats. They didn't even have to wear a cape or hat or anything. It felt very unofficial and awkward to her.

Ben, of course, ate up the applause. As she made her way back to her seat, rolled-up paper in hand that proved she was good enough to stay in Dreadmore, she scanned the crowd of faces for her parents. They were easy to find. Her beaming mother was waving from the fourth row, carrying a camera in the other and pointing it right at Kiera. Her father was seated beside her, slightly scrunched down in his seat due to the crowd being so large. He did grin and wave at her, too, when they made eye contact, though.

After she acknowledged them, she examined the crowd a second time, searching for Ezra's parents. She'd never seen them before and was immensely curious at this point to finally see what they looked like. Would they be threatening, wearing all black and looking down on everyone around them? Would they have a dubious, frightening air about them as Kent did? Or would they look like Ezra, completely normal in clothes and expression?

Unfortunately, the walk to her seat only took ten seconds, so she didn't have enough time to find someone who looked similar to either of the brothers.

After she took a seat, Ben plopped down beside her and whispered into her ear, "You didn't clap for me when I received the diploma. What kind of a friend are you?"

"In case you hadn't noticed, my hands were full with this." She held her own diploma up at him with raised eyebrows. "And I could say the same. Why didn't *you* clap for *me*?"

He crossed his arms and leaned away, crinkling his graduation papers. "I don't clap for people who are beneath me."

Kiera scoffed quietly, keeping up the act of being insulted alongside him, then she actually did clap as Ezra approached the stage.

While he walked back to his seat a few rows down from her, she saw him focus behind her. Curious, she turned around and finally found where his family had been sitting. She'd expected them to take a spot in the front row since they were related to the headmaster, but instead, they were near the back.

The man, presumably Ezra's father, was tall and didn't look like Ezra at all. He had dark hair that curled around his ears and tan skin that was mostly covered up by a brown turtleneck despite the warm summer weather. Rather than looking conceited or judgmental, he looked more tired than anything.

He leaned slightly to the right like he was ready to fall asleep on his wife's shoulder.

Ezra's mother was the one who looked like she was in charge. She sat up straight with both hands clutching a small, pink purse, and she was studying the stage with a critical eye and darting look. Her face was similar to Ezra's, though more feminine and accentuated by light makeup. Her hair was also up in a curled bun with a small pink hat to match her purse. The rest of her body was covered by a prim, black dress that made it look like she should be attending a more formal event.

The pair stood out among all the other couples, who mainly wore casual clothes. However, despite looking somewhat wealthy and very educated, they didn't look evil or harsh. They weren't what Kiera expected, and they didn't scare her like Kent either.

Ezra nodded at both of them before sitting down, but his eyes didn't light up the way they did when he looked at Kiera a second later. He cast her a small smile before disappearing among the crowd of students. Once again, seeing him acknowledge her so brightly filled her with butterflies and an urge to keep him smiling.

As the ceremony came to a close, Kiera stood up and noticed Kent stepping off the stage with the other professors so he could join his parents. Both she and Ben bristled as he walked past. Ben had heard enough about him to be cautious around him.

Once he was gone, Kiera breathed a sigh of relief and turned toward Ben. "So, meet in the parking lot in ten?" They were carpooling today since his parents couldn't make it for the graduation, and they lived so close together that this was just easier. She had already put her clothes from the dorm into the car, too, so all they had to do was pack themselves in and head out.

"Sure, after you say goodbye to your boyfriend, of course," he said. "And I will... say goodbye to Tucker... and his friends."

Kiera stopped what she was doing and squinted at him, wondering why his cheeks were turning red, and he kept pausing between words. Then she glanced over his shoulder at Tucker, who was currently speaking to Sally and Meiying. Ezra was with them too, but he kept glancing at Kiera, so she knew he'd be coming to say goodbye.

"You're just going to say goodbye to Tucker?" she asked slowly, raising an eyebrow and studying both Sally and Meiying. She hadn't noticed Ben getting particularly close to either of the girls before, but his actions had just given him away. "No one else?"

"Of course not," Ben said, his obvious lie unconcealed by his nervous laugh. "Oh look, Ezra's coming over. Time for me to gracefully back out so you two can have a moment alone together." Ben was full-on blushing as he stepped away, and Ezra took his place.

"What's wrong with him?" Ezra whispered as Ben approached Tucker. "He was red in the face."

"I think I know," Kiera whispered, peering past Ezra to see who Ben spoke to first. Sure enough, her best friend took a spot right next to Meiying. His entire body was angled toward her, though they didn't touch and Meiying seemed unaware of it. "I won't say anything until I confirm it, though."

Ezra turned to look, but Kiera grabbed him before he could. "Don't make it obvious."

"Does Ben have a crush on one of the girls?" Ezra asked. "I thought his only love was comic books."

"I thought the same," Kiera said. "But I think that has finally changed.

Ben said something to Meiying, and she laughed.

"I finally have something to tease him about," Kiera whispered with glee.

Ezra looked ready to say something in response, but then Kent called his name, and he sighed.

"I have to go," he said quietly, grabbing both her

arms and pulling her closer. It was so sudden that she didn't have time to think. Then, for just a split second, he leaned forward and kissed her. It was so fast that she didn't have time to process it. Then he said something about seeing her during the summer or at the beach or something, but she wasn't able to recall exactly what it was. She was in too much shock. The last time they kissed was last semester in the heat of a battle, and while she'd thought about kissing him since, she hadn't expected it to be now, right in front of his parents and eldest brother.

"Bye," she whispered as he slipped past her. "Text me!" she called after him, turning to see him go but freezing when both his mother and father's eyes fell on her. They made eye contact for a brief moment, appraising her, then she turned back around. Too much was happening at once. She couldn't process this.

Luckily, her mother ran into her a second later, ranting about how exciting this was, and by the time she turned back around, Ezra and his family were gone.

As she, too, said goodbye to Tucker and his friends, then dragged Ben away from the group so they could return home, she decided she'd investigate Ezra's family a little further over the summer.

That kiss made one thing clear: Ezra didn't plan to give her up just because Kent said she wasn't worth it. If that was the case, she was going to ensure they stayed together. If that involved dealing with Kent and his controlling ways, so be it.

The car ride home was even better than last time, and she looked forward to seeing Ezra again and yet again improving her skills in magic.

Hopefully, by the end of next year, she'd officially have a boyfriend and enrollment into a magic medical school. If she was lucky, there wouldn't be any life-threatening serial killers or fairies to get in her way too. One could only hope.

Click for more Mia Hall books!

Sign up for Mia's Newsletter to find out about releases.
Put the following in your browser window:
mailerlite.com/webforms/landing/e1d4k4